Hers to Redeem
The Reclusive Man

I0620766

Mitchell's

Misfortune

J. L. Dawson

Hers to Redeem
The Reclusive Man

Mitchell's Misfortune

By J L Dawson

Butterfly Books
PUBLISHING

Publisher's Note: This book is a work of fiction. Names, characters, places and incidents are products of the author's imagination or used in a fictional context. All characters are fictional, and any similarity to people living or dead is purely coincidental.

Cover design by: Virginia McKevitt
Edited by: Amber Smith

ISBN (Paperback) 978-1-7385962-2-5
ISBN (E-book) 978-1-7385962-3-2

A CiP catalogue record for this title is available from the National Library of New Zealand.

Edition 18, 2023 Butterfly Books Publishing

Contact the author or subscribe to newsletter:
jldawsonauthor@yahoo.com
www.jodawsonauthor.com

Contents

One

"How long will you be gone?" Miranda Gibson placed both hands on her fiance's chest.

"About a week, maybe more; we have to go further afield to cut enough logs." Mitchell Sullivan smiled and took her into his arms. "It shouldn't be too much longer than that."

"Why do you even have to go? You're a smithy, not a lumberjack?"

Mitchell sighed and brushed her cheek with his knuckles. "I've told you this, if I help them out, they'll give me a discount on the lumber. I have a house to finish, remember?"

"I remember." She pursed her lips comically. "I'll miss you."

"It'll be nice to be missed." Mitchell chuckled. He stroked the soft white cheek of the woman who'd captured his heart and smiled at her. His dark eyes shone his love. "I can't believe I get to marry you in a month."

"I can't wait." Miranda put her arms around his neck and kissed him deeply.

"Phewwww, when you kiss me like that, you make my knees buckle."

"A big strong man like you?"

"I'm only strong on the outside. On the inside, I'm weak as a kitten, unless I have you loving me." He tucked a blonde tress of hair behind her ear and flashed her the toothy smile she loved so much.

"Just as well, I do love you, then."

"Sully, you comin'?" a voice yelled from behind them.

Mitchell turned to look at the men on horseback. "I'll be right there." He grimaced and turned back to Miranda. "I gotta go." He kissed her again, grabbed the bag of food from her hands, and hurried down the stairs. Mitchell leaped on his horse, Blackjack, and followed the group out of town.

Miranda watched until they were out of sight and turned back into the house. She sighed and strolled to the kitchen.

Archie looked up from his breakfast. "He's gone then?"

"Yep."

"He'll be back, Sis."

"I know. I'm just really gonna miss him."

"Throw yourself into wedding planning instead," her father said around a mouthful of pancake. "You're costing me an arm and a leg as it is."

"Pa, you didn't have to say yes to Mitch if you didn't want to pay for a wedding."

Brian Gibson looked up at her and smiled. "I just want you to be happy, Darling. Sullivan's a good chap, hardworking, and I have no problem with the lad. He's the best smithy I've ever known; never seen the likes of some of his designs." He glanced up at a shelf above his son's head with elaborately twisted steel brackets holding it to the wall.

Miranda scooped two pancakes onto her plate and hurried over to join the men. "At least it'll give me time to finish my dress before he comes home so I can keep it secret."

2

Archie frowned. "Why does that matter? I know what Clara's dress looks like."

Miranda shrugged. "I dunno; I just think it'll knock his socks off to see me float up the aisle in my new gown."

Brian gripped her hand. "It sure will, Darling. The light will shine on your lovely golden hair, and you'll look like an angel."

A cough came from opposite her. Both father and daughter's eyes swung to Archie's face.

He flashed them a teasing grin. "Angel's taking it a bit far."

"You'll keep, Archie Gibson." Miranda flicked a blob of butter at her brother, hitting him on the chin.

"Hey." Archie chuckled, wiped the butter off his face with his finger, and put it in his mouth. He became serious then. "You meeting with Clara today?"

"Of course, she's my best friend."

"Handy that. It's good to know my sister and my fiancée are close."

"She was my friend before she became your fiancée." Miranda raised her brows at her brother.

"It was kind of you to befriend my future wife. Sister," he teased.

Miranda shook her head at her older brother. "Just eat your pancakes."

Archie laughed and shoveled a large piece into his mouth.

* * * *

"Good morning, Miss Gibson." Charlie Jones sidled up to Miranda as she walked towards the café in the spring sunshine. He was handsome, suave, and rich.

"Mr. Jones." Miranda blushed. The way he looked at her so admiringly always made her squirm.

"How are you today, Ma'am?"

"Just fine, Mr. Jones. And you?"

"I'm rather down, actually."

She stopped walking and turned to talk to Mitchell's friend. "Oh, and why is that?"

He took her hand and lifted it to his lips. "Because you chose Mitchell and not me. What does he have that I don't?"

Miranda snapped back her hand. This wasn't the first time he'd tried to steal her from Mitchell. "I... I love him."

"You think you do, but I can give you so much more than he can. I've got a large spread, more money, a big house; he's got a tiny cabin and a rundown workshop."

"He's building us a new home at the edge of town."

"I know that, but it's still only half the size of my home. I'm quite wealthy, you know."

"I don't love him for what he has. I love him for who he is."

Charlie ran a hand down her arm and looked her in the eyes. "I think you and I would be good together. You're a lovely woman, Miranda."

"I'm marrying Mitchell, and no amount of you convincing me will change that, Mr. Jones."

He smiled. "Very well." He stroked her cheek and leaned in to whisper in her ear. "But it won't stop me from trying to change your mind. I want you to be my wife, Miss Gibson."

Miranda blushed deeply and swallowed. "Mr. Jones, I've turned you down before, and I'll do so again." She subconsciously twisted her engagement ring. "Every time you ask."

"Very well, I'll admit defeat, for now." He tipped his head to her. "Where are you headed?"

"To the café to meet with Clara."

"Of course. Would you allow me to escort you since your fiancé is away?"

"Sure." She smiled and took his arm; after all, he was an old friend of Mitch's. "It's a beautiful day today."

"Yes, it's beautiful sunshine. It brings out the shine to your lovely hair." Charlie paused outside the café and brushed some hair back from her face.

She blushed and chuckled as he opened the door to the café for her. "Thank you." She smiled and hurried inside.

Clara looked up from her coffee cup as Miranda sat down. "What's that all about?" She frowned.

"Oh, you know he's a friend of Mitch's."

"Be careful there, Mandy; he's charming and rich."

"And I'm not in love with him; I love Mitchell."

"I know." Clara nodded. "Coffee?"

"Yes, of course." Miranda smiled and waved Alice over.

Two

Martin Chadwick ran into the general store. "Quick, there are riders coming in, and fast."

Archie and Brian hurried around the desk. "What is it? Outlaws?"

"No, it's the men that went for the trees."

Brian looked at his son, wide-eyed. "It's only been three days; why are they back?"

"Beats me." Martin shrugged. They heard galloping hooves, and the three men ran outside. A crowd was gathering. Miranda and Clara hurried out of the dress shop and stood amongst the onlookers.

"Doc!" Mathias Ford arrived in town first on horseback; the wagons some ways behind him. "Get the doc."

Doctor Wells hurried out of his clinic. "What is it?" he called, just as the sheriff approached from the other side of the road.

"Logs gave way; three men got crushed. Two dead, one injured."

Many bystanders gasped and looked around anxiously, and murmurs traveled through the gathered crowd.

"Who?" Sheriff Connor stopped as Ford leaped off his horse.

"Tanner and Wright are dead. It's Sully that's injured."

"Ohhhhh!" Miranda gasped and a strong arm reached around her waist. She turned and noticed Mr. Jones standing beside her.

The wagons pulled up, and the doctor ran to the wagon box. "What happened?"

He looked at the men as they prepared to lift Mitchell off on a crude stretcher.

"It's his leg, Doc; he saved Mason and Hicks, pushed them to the side, but got stuck between the logs. His leg is crushed." Ford nodded to the two other men helping with the stretcher. Mason and Hicks wore expressions of gratitude and sorrow.

Mitchell groaned loudly as they passed the stretcher to the men waiting on the ground.

"Quick, get him into the clinic," the doctor directed the men carrying the stretcher.

Sheriff Connor gestured to the Reverend. "Help me with the two bodies."

Reverend Cross nodded and hurried to help.

Sobs and wails rang out, and the crowd moved almost as one to huddle around the clinic door.

"I have to go to him," Miranda sobbed out.

Clara held her hand. "You can't; you need to let the doctor work."

"He'll be okay. Doc Wells is a good doctor." Mr. Jones slipped his arm around her again. She didn't resist him; instead, overwhelmed, she lay her head on his shoulder. "He'll be okay, Miranda, I promise." He slipped both arms around her and did his best to sound caring.

* * * *

"He's coming to." Doctor Wells looked up at his nurse.

Annie Miller put her hand on the man's shoulder. "He's gonna be in a lot of pain when he wakes."

The doctor nodded. "Get the morphine ready. And Annie, I've seen this before. Be prepared for him to be angry. Most people are in his situation."

"I understand, Doctor." She nodded and hurried to the shelf to find the morphine.

Mitchell began to writhe and thrash as his foggy brain registered the pain. He opened his eyes and fought the urge to yell. "Wha... where... what?" he managed through tightly gritted teeth.

Doctor Wells placed his hand on Mitchell's shoulder. "Mr. Sullivan, you're in the clinic. You had an accident with falling logs."

"My leg..." Mitchell groaned. "On fire." Sweat streamed from the man's face, and he continued to thrash. It provided some distraction from the pain.

"Yes, it'll hurt for some time." The doctor took a deep breath. "I had to take your leg off just below the knee."

"What, Doc? You took my leg?" Mitchell was suddenly alert; he tried to sit up and look, but was in too much pain. "But it hurts in my foot; I can feel it. It's on fire."

"That's normal; it's called phantom pains; it'll subside in time."

Mitchell fell back against the pillow, his dark eyes staring at the ceiling as he tried to process the information. He heaved in deep breaths.

"Nurse, give him a dose. We need him to sleep."

"Certainly, Doctor." The nurse emptied a packet of powder into a tin cup of water, stirred it with a spoon, and lifted it to Mitchell's mouth.

8

"No... get that away from me!" He thrust an arm at the cup, knocking it from the nurse's hand and pushing her to the ground. The tin cup hit the floor with a loud thud, spilling liquid across the wooden boards. The nurse rubbed her elbow and stood up, brushing her skirts back into place. The doctor eyed her, to make sure she was okay and turned back to the writhing man.

He tried in vain to hold him down, but Mitchell lashed out in agony. The blacksmith was broad and strong, and the duo struggled to calm him. "Get me some help!" the doctor yelled. "We gotta get pain relief into him." Annie nodded and hurried out the door.

"Calm down, Mr. Sullivan. Please, I'll give you some pain relief, but you need to calm down." He spoke in his soothing, professional voice.

"No, get away from me!" Mitchell continued to thrash; anything to distract his mind from the agony.

Three men came running in with the nurse and working together; they managed to hold Mitchell down. The doctor picked up the large syringe he used for inoculations and filled it with liquid painkiller. "Hold him down."

The men pushed tightly against Mitchell's shoulders and arms while the doctor administered the pain relief in his upper arm. Mitchell cried out loudly as the needle pierced his skin. He continued to writhe and sweat and cry out for a time until he slowly calmed.

When at last he stilled, the men backed away, and the doctor nodded his thanks. "He'll sleep now. I'll keep an eye on him. Thank you, Gentlemen."

"You're welcome," Miles Taylor said on the men's behalf, and they left.

"You go on home, Annie; I'll watch him."

"Are you sure, Doctor?"

"Yeah, he'll wake a few times, but I'll be fine from here."

Miranda stood outside the clinic, listening to the cries of the man she loved. Every scream from Mitchell made her heart leap. "He's dying, isn't he? He's going to die." She wept. Charlie Jones hugged her close. Her father and brother sat nearby with Clara. Brian frowned as he watched Charlie embrace Miranda, but he trusted his daughter and knew this man was Mitchell's friend and he wouldn't hurt her, he hoped.

The cries stopped, and the men walked out. Mr. Bonner approached Miranda. Charlie stood with his hand on her elbow. "Doctor says you can go in now."

"Thank you, Mr. Bonner."

The man nodded and hurried away.

Miranda headed inside with Charlie following. "Doctor?"

Doctor Wells looked up from the basin where he was washing his instruments. "Oh, Miss Gibson." He grabbed a nearby towel and dried his hands and forearms. He rolled down his sleeves as he walked to her.

"How is he?" Tears sat on her cheeks.

The doctor did up the button at his cuff and put a hand on her shoulder. "He's going to be okay, eventually. He's in a lot of pain, so I'm keeping him sedated."

"What's wrong with him, Doctor? Why was he screaming?"

The doctor looked her in the eye. "You don't know?"

"Know what?"

"I had to take off his leg. Just below the knee."

Miranda felt a punch to her stomach. She buckled at the knees, and Charlie picked her up and carried her to a chair; he held her as she cried. "Noooo. No... Not Mitchell... Nooo!"

She eventually calmed and sat back from Charlie. He handed her his handkerchief, and she dried her eyes.

"Doctor, can I see him?" She stood and swallowed.

"Yes, come on, I'll take you to him."

Charlie followed Miranda, and the doctor into the last recovery room. Mitchell was asleep in the bed. He looked so peaceful. Miranda fell into the chair next to him. "Oh, my darling." She kissed his forehead and gripped his hand. Charlie sat in the chair beside her, placing his hand on her back. "My darling." Miranda sobbed and lay her head on Mitchell's forehead. She looked down at the bed and noticed the blankets sitting flat where his left lower leg should be. She broke down in sobs again, lying her head on his chest. Charlie rubbed his hand up and down her back but didn't say a word.

*   *   *   *

"Mir... Miran... Mir..." Mitchell opened his eyes and lifted a hand to touch Miranda, lying across his chest. His foggy brain registered the pain again, and he

11

exhaled loudly and gritted his teeth, fighting the urge to scream.

Miranda woke up. "Ohhh. Oh, my darling."

"Miranda..." he managed, exhaling loudly. He fought to hide his agony, not wanting to frighten her. He moved his head and noticed Charlie Jones sitting next to her, his hand on her back. He was asleep in his chair with his chin on his chest.

Mitchell groaned, and Miranda gripped his hand and stroked his brow. "Oh, Darling. Are you hurting?"

He gritted his teeth and nodded.

"Oh, I'll get the doctor." She leaped up and hurried out of the room.

Charlie woke up abruptly with a snort as Miranda left. "Jones..."

Charlie stood up and feigned a worried look. "How are you, my friend?" He put his hand on Mitchell's shoulder.

"Pain..." Mitchell exhaled loudly.

The doctor hurried in with Miranda. "How are you feeling, Mr. Sullivan?"

Mitchell gritted his teeth. Sweat ran from his forehead, and the doctor nodded. He reached for another pouch of morphine and stirred it into a glass, lifting Mitchell's head to help him drink. "That'll take a few minutes to kick in; just hang in there, Mitch."

Mitchell nodded, clenched his teeth and gripped the sides of the bed until his knuckles turned white. Miranda clung to his arm and wept silently. At last, his breathing calmed, and the doctor wiped his brow.

"Thanks, Doc." Mitchell exhaled loudly through his teeth. The pain hadn't gone away but was bearable.

12

"You're welcome. I don't want to give you any more morphine than that because it's easy to get addicted to."

Mitchell nodded. "I understand." He closed his eyes. "What am I supposed to do now?"

"What do you mean?" Miranda wiped at a tear that traced down his cheek.

"I mean, I got one leg... can't do much with one leg." He clenched his jaw against the rising anger and fear he felt. "Ain't much of a man...." His voice petered out.

Miranda closed her eyes and trembled, embarrassed to note that the voice inside her agreed with him. *That's not how I really feel. Is it?* She tucked her lips inwards.

Doctor Wells gripped Mitch's shoulder and pulled up the chair beside him. "Mr. Sullivan, I know you're angry and frustrated. I want you to know I did everything possible to save your leg, but it was crushed beyond repair. Taking your leg saved your life. You know two other men didn't make it."

Mitchell closed his eyes. "Who?"

"Wright and Tanner."

"What about Coop and Max? I pushed 'em away when I saw the logs start to roll."

"They made it; they were the ones that brought you in," Charlie offered; Mitchell noticed him rub Miranda's back again and grimaced.

"To answer your question, Mr. Sullivan, you can do plenty. There's been a lot of progress in prosthetics since the war. I can order you something, and you'll adjust to it."

Mitchell gritted his teeth. "Prosthetics?"

"Artificial limbs."

Mitchell sighed. "In time to get married in a month?" His eyes flicked to Miranda's.

She lowered her head and tucked her lips under again. Mitchell caught it but said nothing.

"You'll be up by then but far from healed. You could get married as long as you're careful, and Miranda will have to see to your wound for several months and be diligent, so infection doesn't set in; even after it's healed, there'll be sores and pain to adjust to, and the artificial limb."

Miranda's head snapped up; she tried hard to keep the horror out of her eyes. "For how long?"

The doctor shrugged. "Recovery will take a good three-four months before he's really back on his feet, maybe longer, perhaps half a year." He grimaced. "Unfortunate turn of phrase, but you know what I mean."

"Months?" Miranda looked worried. "But, what about us, our marriage?"

"What about it?" Mitchell squinted at her and raised a hand to her cheek. "I'll be needing you more than ever now, Darling. But I'll get through this." He clenched his square jaw determinedly. "You'll see. We'll get through this together."

Miranda turned her lips in and gave him a single nod, and Charlie rubbed his hand up her back. A twinge of fear began to rise in Mitchell's mind.

* * * *

14

"Good to see you sitting up." Mr. Gibson and his son were the latest visitors in a steady stream. "That's pretty good after only a few days."

"The rest of me is fine, Sir. As long as the doc gives me pain relief, I'm okay for the most part." Mitchell tried to remain positive. But in the long hours he spent alone, his mind ran away with him. He'd finally convinced Miranda to go and get some sleep. She'd wept a lot, and he knew she was exhausted.

"That's good. You'll be up around before you know it." Archie nodded.

Mitchell shrugged. "And then what?"

"What do you mean? Then you and Miranda will get married like you planned, and you'll return to work."

Mitchell raised his brows at Brian. "You don't mind having a cripple for a son-in-law?"

Brian frowned at him. "You aren't a cripple. And your mind and heart are not changed, are they? Plenty of men lose a leg and can still provide for their families. The war caused a lot of similar injuries, and those men learn to adjust."

Mitch shrugged. "Yeah, but we'll have to delay the wedding?"

"How come?" Archie sat back in his chair and crossed his arms.

"'Cause I'll be outta action for several months, and I can't finish the house in this state...."

"Don't worry about that, Son; we'll get a crew there to finish it for you. Have it ready for Miranda and you. Then you can get better in your own home with your wife to take care of you."

Mitchell gave Brian a wry smile. "I hope she'll still want to marry me now that I'll have a peg leg."

"What kind of thing is that to say?" The older man grimaced. "Course she will. For better or worse, remember?"

"We aren't married yet." Mitch scratched his chin and sighed, the foreboding worry mounting in his mind.

Brian stood and gripped his shoulder. "It'll work out just fine, don't you worry."

"Thanks." Mitchell sighed. He'd accepted this was his lot now; not a whole lot else he could do but accept it. The timing was awful; just as he and Miranda were about to begin their lives together, she would be lumped with a wounded husband. "You better get going back to work." He gestured to the clock.

"You're right. Good to see you looking a bit brighter. We'll be praying for you."

"Hmm, for what it's worth," Mitchell muttered as the two left the room.

Three

"Hold on to me." Brian and Archie stood on either side of Mitchell and linked their arms around his shoulders to help him up.

Miranda gulped as he pulled the blanket away, allowing the men to help him stand. His pinned-up trouser leg made her gasp without meaning to. She turned her eyes away with the excuse of fetching his crutches. Passing them to him, she managed a shaky smile.

He flashed her his grin. "Thank you, Darling." He tucked the crutches under his armpits and leaned his weight on them.

"Ya steady?" the doctor asked.

"I'll help him, Doc; we'll get him home," Brian promised.

"I'll be over to check on you tomorrow, and Miranda can keep up with checking on your wounds." Doctor Wells smiled at her, and Mitchell nodded his thanks.

Miranda turned her back to open the door, and a slight shudder ran through her. *What was that? Why do you feel this way? You love him!*

With Brian and Archie's help, Mitchell hobbled out to the waiting wagon. They assisted him up into the back; and he sat with his legs propped up on pillows. Miranda and Archie sat on each side of him in case the morphine made him too woozy, and he'd fall.

At last, with great effort, they had Mitch back in his little cabin and his own bed. Sweat poured down his face again, and he gritted his teeth against the pain.

"You, okay?" Brian asked.

"Yeah," Mitchell hissed out. "I swear I can feel my foot; it's burning."

"Doc says that's normal, phantom pains. Could last a few days, weeks, or even months."

"Oh, great." Mitchell grimaced.

"You want some morphine?"

"Nah, Doc said I could only have so much a day; too easy to become addicted. I can bear it for now."

"Okay, you need anything?" Archie glanced at the clock.

"Nah, you go back to work; I'll be fine. Miranda will take care of me, I'm sure." Mitchell grinned at her, standing in the doorway.

She gave him a hesitant smile.

"Very good; we'll come by and visit you tomorrow, Son." Brian gripped his shoulder.

Mitchell nodded his thanks to both men, and they headed out the door. Miranda followed them to the front door. "What am I supposed to do?"

Brian frowned. "What do you mean?"

"I'm not a nurse; I don't know 'bout sick people."

"Mitch isn't sick. He's just in pain. He'll be up and around on his crutches in no time; it's important that he doesn't get an infection. So see to his wounds each day like the doc showed you."

She grimaced internally but plastered on a smile and nodded. Stepping back inside she hung her head, and sighed loudly. *Come on, Miranda,* she chastened herself and hurried into his room, her smile firmly held in place. "You comfortable?"

"Could you hand me another pillow?"

"Sure." She snatched a couple from the couch in the living area. "Here you go." She pushed them down behind his back. "Doc said you should sit up as much as possible, so you don't get bedsores. And you can be up and around a bit more." Her voice trembled.

Finally, she sat on the chair beside the bed. Mitchell looked at her trembling lips and frightened eyes. "Miranda?"

She looked up at him. "Yes?"

"What's the matter?"

She smiled politely. "Oh, nothing, I'm fine. I'm just worried about you, I guess."

Mitchell shrugged. "I'm still me. Leg or no leg, I'm still me."

"I know that."

He squinted at her. "Then how come you can barely look at me, and barely touch me?"

She took a deep breath, and tears sprang to the corners of her eyes. "It's nothing, really; I'm sorry, Mitch. I think I just got a fright seeing you with your trousers pinned up."

"Doesn't bother you, does it?" He crossed his arms.

"Bother me?"

"That I lost a leg?"

"Oh... um... no, it doesn't bother me exactly...."

Mitch furrowed his brows and scratched his chin. "That didn't sound convincing. What's the problem? Are you ashamed of me now?"

"I... I dunno, I guess I just aren't cut out to be a nursemaid."

His eyebrows flew up. "I thought you loved me?"

"Of course, I do."

"But you can't bear to help me, see to my wounds for a few weeks?" He grimaced.

"Mitchell, you know I love you; it's just this isn't what I expected for our marriage."

"The wedding is supposed to be next week, Miranda. I've been working hard for the last three weeks to be up and about so we could still get married." He raised his brows again. "You do still want to get married, don't ya?"

Miranda felt her heart race and pound in her ears. She turned her lips under and looked down.

Mitchell leaned over and raised her chin. "Miranda. You still want to get married, don't ya?"

"I don't know," she said in a small voice.

A knife stabbed at Mitchell's heart, a pain worse than his leg. "What do you mean? You either want to get married, or you don't?"

She stood up and walked over to look out the room's one small window. She looked past Mitchell's smithy shop towards town, noticing Mr. Jones walk up the boardwalk across the street. He'd offered her to marry him several times since Mitch's accident. She sighed loudly.

"Miranda." Mitchell painfully made his way out of bed; leaning on his crutches, he hobbled over to her. He reached out a hand to turn her around. "I love you. I need you. Now more than ever."

"Oh, Mitchell." Her eyes filled with tears. "I love you; I really do; it's just...."

He scowled and nodded. "You can't marry a cripple?"

She sighed loudly and put a hand on his arm. A slight tremble ran through her. "You aren't a cripple, and I feel so bad feeling the way I do. I'm sorry for you, I really am...."

"No, ya aren't." He cut her off and sat back on the windowsill to take the weight off his good leg.

"What do you mean?" Her lips trembled, and large tears fell from her eyes.

"You aren't sorry for me, and you don't really love me." His dark eyes fixed on her face.

"How can you say that? Of course, I love you."

"No, you don't, 'cause if you did, you wouldn't hesitate when I asked if you wanna marry me. You wouldn't cringe every time you saw my leg; you wouldn't look away when I hobble or trip. For better or worse, Mir." He grimaced.

"Oh, Mitchell, I do love you...."

Mitchell put a hand up to stop her. He gripped the crutch under his armpit and lifted his hand to stroke her cheek. He fixed dark eyes on hers. "I love you, Mir. If you lost a leg or both legs and arms, I'd never leave your side. I'd wait on you every moment for the rest of my days. I'd do whatever I could to make your life better and ease the pain. But I'd never doubt my love for you;

I'd never be embarrassed to be seen with you. If you had burns all over your face or turned green, I would still love you, no matter what. Your happiness is all that matters to me. That's how I know you don't love me. Something as trivial as a leg wouldn't make a scrap of difference if you really loved me."

Miranda turned to look out the window; her hands over her face, weeping heavily. Mitchell reached his arm out to her and drew her into an embrace. Despite his heart bleeding, he couldn't bear to see her cry.

Finally, she pulled back from him; but wouldn't look him in the eye. Mitchell lifted her chin again. "I'll ask you again. Miranda Gibson, I love you. Do you still wanna get married in a week's time?"

Miranda lifted soft blue eyes to him, and her lips trembled. She shook her head ever so slightly. "I'm sorry," she sobbed out.

"Miranda." Mitchell fell back onto the bed, and his crutches hit the floor with a loud thud.

"I'm sorry," she said again, in a tiny voice. She slid the engagement ring off her finger, sat it on his armoire, and hurried out of the room.

Mitchell sat with both hands grasping the bed on either side of him. He stared at the floor for some time, and darkness filled his soul. *So, God has forsaken me.*

Miranda ran outside and sped past the smithy shop. Reaching the side wall of the mercantile, she paused, leaned against the wall, and broke down in loud sobs.

Charlie Jones had been walking back and forth up the street. He knew she'd be out sooner or later, and he hoped to convince her to ditch that cripple and be with him instead. He'd asked her several times, and just in the last week, he'd felt her resolve begin to crumble and knew it wouldn't take much persuading.

Charlie wandered past the mercantile and heard someone sobbing. He despised emotional women, so he gingerly peered around the corner to make a hasty retreat if needed. He gasped. "Mir?" Taking a deep breath, he sucked back his annoyance. *This is my chance, while she's vulnerable, she'll be putty in my hands.*

He walked over and took her in his arms, cradling her head. "There, there, Darling, whatever is the matter?"

Miranda sobbed for some time, clinging to Charlie. Finally, she calmed, and he passed her his handkerchief. *Great, now it'll be covered in tears.* He grimaced and gave her a false smile. "What's the matter?" He brushed away a tear she'd missed.

"I just broke off my engagement with Mitchell." Her voice was low, and she shook.

"Oh." He raised his brows, trying to come across as compassionate. *That's the best news yet; time to swoop.* "It must have been a misunderstanding, surely?"

"No." She shook her head and lifted her hand so he could see. "I gave him back the ring."

"Oh, Darling." He embraced her again and rubbed her back. "I'm so sorry." She calmed, and he pointed towards the common and the wooden chair under the oak.

She nodded and took his offered arm. Charlie led her to the seat, sat beside her, put his arm around her, and gently guided her head to his shoulder. "Care to tell me why?"

Miranda shrugged. "I don't want to sound petty."

"You could never sound petty, Miranda; you are the least petty, most caring woman I know."

"I couldn't be his nursemaid. And I... Oh, I'm so ashamed of myself...."

"Whatever for?"

"I couldn't marry him now. I love him, but I'm just not cut out to be married to a...."

He raised his brows. "A cripple?"

She let out a sob. "He isn't a cripple, but he is rather unfortunate now. I feel so horrible; I know he needs me more than ever, but I'm just not cut out to be a nursemaid."

Charlie took her in his arms and rocked her gently. "I understand. Of course, you aren't. You're meant to be a kept woman, the lady of an estate." He uttered flattering words to her and stroked her back. "Much too lovely and beautiful to be a nurse to an old cripple all your days."

At long last, she stopped crying and sat back. Charlie gently wiped away a tear from her cheek. "You are so lovely, Miranda."

She gave him a shy smile. The intensity of his gaze made her heart pound. He rubbed her arm and stared into her eyes. Slowly he lowered his head until her lips were on his. She didn't resist him, so he continued the kiss.

He broke it off and stroked her cheek. "I really think you should be with me instead of him."

"What are you saying?"

"You were planning to marry anyway; why not marry me? You don't have to wait for a house to be ready; we can get married immediately and move in today."

"But, I...."

"What?" He stroked her cheek again. "I want you to be my wife, Miranda. Come on; we can get married right now."

"But my father, my brother?"

"What about them? You don't need their approval. You're a grown woman; you know your own heart."

"They're my family."

"They'll still be your family, and you'll have me." He smiled at her and stroked her cheek again. He stood and pulled her up with him. Taking her in his arms, he kissed her again, this time holding the kiss even longer. He felt her melt into his arms, and knew she was his. "What say you, Miranda? Marry me?"

"Okay." Her cheeks colored deeply.

"Yes." He lifted his hand to her cheek. "Come on, let's go to the reverend now."

"We don't have a ring."

"Yes, I do." He reached into his breast pocket and pulled out a ring with a large diamond on top.

"You just happened to have that with you?" She raised her brows at him.

"I knew you'd say yes to me sooner or later. I wanted to be prepared." He lifted her hand and slid it on her finger. "That's the most expensive engagement ring in this town." He kissed her again, pulling her tightly against himself. Finally pulling back from her, he grinned and took her hand. "Come on, let's not wait. We can be married right away and get on with our life together. You'll be an excellent lady of the manor."

Swept away in overwhelming emotion, she allowed herself to be led.

Four

"...I now pronounce you man and wife."

Charlie grinned and grabbed Miranda; pulling her close, he kissed her passionately. The reverend and his wife, the only witnesses, frowned as the man's hands began to rove immediately. When he finally broke the kiss, Miranda's face was red, and her lips quivered. A slight shiver of regret washed over her. That kiss wasn't like the tender ones they'd shared earlier. This one had an aggressiveness, a possessiveness that worried her. *Surely, it's just the passion of the moment.* She swallowed. Guilt and regret passed through her; how would she ever tell her father?

But Charlie had already thought of that. He snatched the marriage license from the reverend, nodded his thanks, gripped Miranda's hand, and hurried her out of the church.

"Where are we going?"

"To see your father."

"Ohhhh." She shuddered, anxiety washed over her.

"Miranda?" Brian looked up to see Charlie walk in, holding Miranda's hand. Her face flushed, and her lip trembled. Mr. Gibson furrowed his brows. "What is the meaning of this? Why aren't you with Mitchell?"

"She's no longer engaged to Mitchell, Mr. Gibson. She's my wife." Charlie smirked and looked him in the eye.

Archie dropped his broom and hurried over. Mr. Gibson raised his brows and leaned his head in towards them. "She's your what?" He'd never trusted Charlie. For starters, he was ten years older than Miranda and had always been much too familiar with her.

Charlie grinned, pulled Miranda close with one arm, and thrust the marriage license at her father. "We're legally married. She's my wife."

Mr. Gibson snatched at the piece of paper and looked at his daughter's trembling face and regret in her eyes. He perused the marriage license. "Is this what you want, Miranda?" He seethed internally; sure this man had been dishonest.

"Of course, it is. I didn't force her," Charlie insisted. "Tell them, Darling. Tell them I didn't force you."

"He didn't force me." Her voice was quiet and full of emotion.

"And this is what you want?"

Charlie glared at her, and she knew not to disappoint him. She looked at her father and nodded.

"What about Mitch?" Archie asked.

"What about him?" Charlie was doing a lot of answering on her behalf.

"Miranda, you can't leave Mitch now. The man just lost his leg. I thought you loved him." Archie furrowed his brows.

"I do...." A squinting glare from Charlie. "I mean, I did. I just couldn't marry him...." She began to weep again.

Charlie took over. "She deserves to be with a man who can take care of her, not some useless cripple. Do you really want your daughter having to play nursemaid to some cripple all her life?"

"He's not a cripple. He's healing, and then he'll get an artificial leg and be able to work again. He needs your help now. Miranda, is this really what you want?" Her father held out the marriage license and searched her face.

She said nothing, just looked at the floor.

"Well, Father, Brother." Charlie gave them both arrogant smiles and tipped his hat. "If you don't mind, I think I'm going to take my wife home, and then she can learn what it means to be a wife to a wealthy man rather than a cripple."

Brian didn't like the way Charlie said that. He gripped Miranda's hand. "Are you sure?"

"We need to go." Charlie tried to pull her away.

"Can I have a moment with my daughter? I never got to give her away. I'd just like a moment."

"Very well." Charlie squinted. "I'll be right out on the step. You have five minutes; then I'm coming back for you, Wife."

She nodded. Charlie walked out, and Brian put his arm around Miranda. "What is this all about? Did he force you?"

"No." She shook her head.

"This can't be what you want?" Archie touched her hand. "Him, he's vile; how can you drop Mitchell for the likes of him? I thought you loved Mitch?"

"I do, but I can't be his nursemaid; that's not what a marriage is supposed to be."

Brian raised his brows. "What happened to 'for better or worse'?"

She shrugged and looked at her feet.

Archie screwed his face up at her. "Then you never loved him. I could never break with Clara, even if she lost both eyes and had no teeth. I love her, no matter what."

"That's what Mitch said to me."

"Is this really the best you can do? We can get your marriage annulled," Brian offered.

"That won't be necessary." Charlie strode back in. "Come on. It's time we go home, Wife."

"I won't let you take her." Brian held her hand.

"There is nothing you can do; she isn't yours anymore. She's my wife, she signed here in her own hand. She belongs to me now." Charlie felt her tremble.

Archie groaned at the 'belongs to me' comment.

What have I done? Miranda chastened herself.

"If you're sure this is what you want, Miranda?" Brian raised his brows.

She lowered her head and nodded, then raised her eyes to Charlie and gave him a less-than-convincing smile.

"See, I told you so. We're married. She's my wife, and I'm taking her home." Charlie turned on his heels, holding Miranda tightly by the shoulders. He led her out.

Brian looked at Archie and ran his fingers through his hair. "I don't like the looks of this."

"Me either. But she says he didn't force her. She's eighteen years old; she's made her choice." Archie shrugged.

"I just hope she doesn't live to regret it. I can't believe she broke with Mitch just because he's lost a leg."

"I think I should go to him, Pa, he's gonna need some help, and he doesn't deserve to hear about this through town gossip."

"Go, Son, I'll hold down the fort. Not a very busy day anyway."

*   *   *   *

Archie rapped on the door of Mitchell's cabin. There was no response. He peered in the window and saw Mitch sitting on the chair in front of the fire staring into the flames.

He pushed open the door and walked in. "Mitch."

"Yeah," came Mitch's gruff response; he turned the engagement ring round and round in his large hand.

Archie fell into the chair beside him. "I'm sorry about Miranda."

"She told you she broke with me? Can't bear to nurse a cripple; she doesn't want to be with half a man."

"She didn't say that."

"I still hope she might change her mind. I love her, Arch."

Archie sighed and hung his head. Mitchell swung his eyes to look at his friend. "What?"

"I don't know how to tell you this."

Mitch raised his brows in question.

"She's married."

"What? What do you mean? She only left here a couple of hours ago?"

"I know. But she's married."

Mitch squinted into the flames. "Who?"

Archie shook his head.

"It's Jones, ain't it? He's had his eyes on her for some time. I bet he coerced her into it," Mitchell hissed through his teeth.

"She said she married him willingly." Archie shrugged.

Mitch exhaled loudly. Burying the burning hurt deep in his heart, he sneered, "She's better off anyway. Can't do much now that I'm a cripple."

"Mitch, you ain't a cripple. Your leg is healing; then you'll get a prosthesis and return to work."

"Yeah, but I'll never be the same." He shrugged. "I'm not a whole man anymore. People don't look at me the same as it is. I can't say I blame her."

"For what it's worth, Pa and I are sorry. We do not like that man, but she's of age, and it's her choice." Archie stood. "I'll be by to see ya."

"Why? I ain't gonna be your brother-in-law anymore. Why do ya care?"

"I liked you before you were going to be my brother-in-law, Mitch; I hope you'll still consider me a friend, despite what my sister did."

"Yeah." Mitchell shrugged. "Ain't your fault."

"Good. We'll tell the doc to keep an eye on ya. I really am sorry you ain't gonna be my brother-in-law."

"Thanks."

Archie squeezed the man's shoulder and left.

Mitchell stared into the fire momentarily, then let out a loud guttural groan and threw the engagement ring into the flames. He covered his face with his large hand and broke down in sobs.

Five

"Miranda."

"Morning, Pa." Miranda gave her father a shaky smile.

"How are you, Dear?" Brian embraced her.

"We're doing okay."

He squinted at her. "Is that husband of yours treating you right?"

"He's fine; he doesn't even really see much of me." She shrugged.

"Sis." Archie came over and embraced her. "How are you?"

"Why are you both looking at me like that? I'm not an invalid, and I'm just fine."

"We haven't seen you for over a week, Darling; we're just concerned about you. Charlie Jones isn't exactly the kindest of men."

"Don't talk about him that way. Regardless of what you think of him, he's my husband." She gulped.

"Are you happy?" Brian examined her face.

Miranda smiled and shrugged. "I guess. It's a lovely home and farm. And Charlie leaves me alone most of the time."

"So, what do you do with your time?" Archie wasn't convinced.

She shrugged. "The same as all wives, I cook, clean, garden, and take care of my husband."

There was no blush of a new bride. Miranda looked to have aged five years in a short time. She wasn't sad necessarily, just resigned to her fate.

In all reality, there wasn't a day that went by that she didn't regret marrying Charlie. He wasn't awful; he didn't strike her, at least not often. And she didn't even see him most of the time.

He didn't usually let her come to town, but she'd begged him to let her do some shopping and visit her family. But Charlie was in the town nearby, so she wouldn't dare loiter.

"I have to get my groceries." She looked at her brother, smiled at her father, and walked away.

Archie lunged after her. "Wait, Miranda. Have you seen Mitchell?"

She turned to look at her brother. Her lips quivered, and tears filled her eyes. She shook her head.

He raised his brows. "I think you need to talk to him; it's only fair."

"I don't think I can."

Archie squinted at her. "Then you never really loved him. If you can be so cold and bitter toward him. That man is in agony; if his leg wasn't bad enough, you tore his heart out. I think the least you could do is give him an explanation."

A solitary tear streaked down her cheek, and her lip shook. She lowered her head. "I don't think I can talk to him."

Archie lifted her chin. "Miranda, the man deserves to hear from you."

She merely nodded and hurried away to finish her shopping.

* * * *

"Why do you want to go and see him? You're my wife, not his!" Charlie frowned.

"Today was supposed to be our wedding day. I think I owe him some sort of explanation." Miranda tried desperately to keep the tears at bay, they were standing on the boardwalk, and she didn't want to make a scene.

"You aren't going to let this go, are you?"

"No, I just want to talk to him. I won't be long, but my brother is right; Mitchell deserves to hear it from me. The man is hurting."

Charlie groaned and squeezed the arm he held much tighter than he should've. Miranda's face curled up in pain. "Fine," he sneered. "But I'm coming with you."

"Why?"

"To make sure he doesn't try to hurt you. Or try to take you from me. I don't trust him."

"He's not the one that did either of those things," she murmured, and studied her shoes.

Charlie squinted and lifted her chin, holding it tightly between his finger and thumb. "Watch how you speak to me, Miranda, or I'll show you what happens to wives who disobey."

Miranda gasped. She looked up at him with scared eyes and nodded. "Please let me go. I want to talk to Mitchell alone. Please."

He released her, and she rubbed her chin. "Why?" He squinted his eyes at her.

"I told you. He deserves to hear it from me."

"You still care for him, don't you?"

She nodded and looked away.

He lifted her head again. "So, is our marriage just a sham?"

Miranda fixed her eyes on him. "Let's not pretend our marriage is about love. You've never said that word to me even one time. You give your dog more complements than me."

"There's more to a marriage than love. I care for you."

"Do you?"

"Of course. I wouldn't have married you if I didn't care."

"Is that why you married me? I thought it was so you could have a housekeeper."

He squinted and pulled his hand back to slap her but realized he was in a public place and stopped himself. He leaned in and whispered. "I won't have your impertinence. I'm the husband. You do as I say. I told you, I care about you. Yes, you're a housekeeper; and you're gonna give me some sons. That's why I need you."

Miranda nodded. She was still determined. "Please let me speak to Mitchell. I won't be long."

He growled again. "Fine. I'll be waiting right out front, though. You have half an hour."

"It's okay; I can walk over. I'll meet you at the café afterward if you like?" She smiled kindly at him.

"Fine." He nodded. She thrust her basket at him and hurried away before he could change his mind.

* * * *

36

"It's healing nicely, Mr. Sullivan." Doctor Wells inspected the wound. "I'm confident now that we've kept infection at bay."

Mitchell nodded as the doctor rewrapped the stump. "Thanks, Doc."

"You're much more mobile now, I see; that's great. How's the pain?"

"Bearable."

The doctor gripped his shoulder. "You're coping well."

"Physically, not sure 'bout my soul." Mitchell sighed loudly and grimaced.

"I'm sorry 'bout Miranda."

Mitchell nodded and sucked in the emotion. He needed to change the subject before he got overwhelmed again. "How long before I can get a leg?"

"It'll be another month, at least. The wound has to be completely healed and all the swelling gone so we can mold the leg to fit you. It'll take a trip to the hospital in Ravensfield."

"In the meantime, can I go back to work? I got projects piling up."

The doctor scratched his chin. "I think you ought to give it another week. If you get anything in that wound, it could set you back months. I'll check on you in a few days, and we can see how we go from there. In the meantime, Annie will come over twice a day to clean and wrap the wound. We have the best chance of full healing if we keep it clean and wrapped."

"Thanks, Doc. Much obliged to ya."

"Thank you, Mitchell. I'm grateful that you've forgiven me for taking your leg."

Mitchell shrugged. "It's just a leg. You did what you could. I'm not gonna waste my hate on you."

"Well, I better get back to the clinic."

"Thanks, Doc."

They both spun their heads to look at the door. Someone was knocking. "I'll get it for you." The doctor jumped up.

"Thanks, Doc." Mitchell pulled his trouser leg back down over the wrapped stump and pinned it up.

"Oh, Miranda." Doctor Wells gasped.

Mitchell closed his eyes and sighed.

"Hi, Doc; I was wondering if I might speak to Mitch?"

The doctor turned to look at Mitchell; his eyebrows raised in question.

"Yeah." Mitch sighed and gave him a nod.

"Very well, Mrs. Jones, come on in."

Mitchell grimaced at the mention of her married name. He took a deep breath and forced down the pain deep in his gut, as she stepped inside. The doctor hurried away and closed the door behind him.

Miranda walked in. "Hello, Mitchell."

"Mrs. Jones. What brings you here?" Mitchell's voice was terse and bitter.

Miranda nodded, and her lips trembled. "May I sit?"

He merely shrugged and nodded to the chair opposite.

They both sat in silence for a time. Mitch looked at her and squinted. "Why'd you come here?"

"I wanted to speak to you?"

"Does your husband know you're here?" He spat the word husband.

"Yes."

Another silence. "You wanted to speak."

"I don't really know what to say?" Miranda's eyes glistened with tears.

"Start with why you couldn't tell me you were marrying my former friend."

"Oh, Mitch, I never wanted to hurt you."

Mitchell's eyes narrowed. "Didn't you?"

"Of course not. I loved you."

"No, you didn't. If you loved me, we'd be getting married today." He gulped.

"I don't know how to explain it to you...."

"That you prefer his fortune over my misfortune."

"I'm not as shallow as all that." Her tears spilled over.

"Really? You just prefer not to be married to a cripple."

"Mitch, that's not fair."

"What do you want me to say, Miranda? I love you. I'll always love you. You could lose all of your limbs, and it wouldn't stop me from loving you. None of that should ever matter if you truly love someone. That's how I know you never loved me. You couldn't even give me the courtesy of telling me yourself that you were married to him."

Miranda wept heavily. She stood to leave. "I am sorry."

Mitchell pushed himself up into a standing position and gripped his crutch. He hopped over to her. "Not nearly as sorry as I am." He looked at her intensely. "Are you happy, at least? All I want is for you to be happy. If he makes you happy, then I'll let it go."

She looked at him and tucked her lips under.

"Are you happy?" he asked again.

"I don't know."

He sighed and put his arm out to pull her close. He kissed her hair. "I'm truly sorry, Miranda. I'll never stop loving you."

Feeling his arm around her again was bliss. Charlie hadn't embraced her once since the day they'd got married. Regret and sorrow ran through her, and she began to weep heavily. Mitch held her for a few moments. She stood back from him, looked up, and kissed his cheek. "I have to go." She hurried out the door.

Mitch stood and watched her retreat; he flinched as the door slammed shut behind her. He hung his head and sighed loudly.

Six

Mitchell hobbled out to his forge. He paused for a moment to rub his leg. The wooden limb was heavy, and his leg ached by the end of the day. He groaned loudly, wiped his arm across his forehead, and bent over to continue beating the metal into a curve to make yet another horseshoe. It was tedious, but they were his bread and butter.

He much preferred making iron gates or ornamental baskets for flowers, working with wrought iron and turning it into beautiful sculptures. He sighed loudly and wiped more sweat from his face. It was hot and heavy work, but he was grateful to have his own business.

"Sullivan!" a voice called. He let out a guttural groan, put down his tongs, hammer, and horseshoe, removed his thick gloves, and hobbled toward the man.

Leaning against the corral rail, Mitchell raised his brows to the man standing before him. "What do you want, Murphy?"

"That ain't no way to treat a paying customer."

Mitchell sighed loudly and gritted his teeth. "What can I do for you, Mr. Murphy?" He plastered on the sweetest smile he could muster.

"Much better. I've broken my cattle brand. I'm just wondering if you can repair it." The man held it up. The hanging R had snapped in half, and the side of the circle was mangled.

Mitchell took the blackened steel and turned it over in his large hands. He frowned. "How'd that happen?"

"Got trodden on by the herd. One of my men left it out."

Mitchell shrugged. "Yeah, I can fix this; I might have to rebuild the R rather than joining it."

"Whatever you think is best. You do good work with metal."

Mitchell gave him a nod; he thought of the lineup of projects he had waiting for him. "Have it for you by Friday."

Murphy gritted his teeth. "I was hoping to get it tomorrow."

"Everyone wants their job done by tomorrow. It's not a quick fix. You're welcome to come and do it yourself," Mitch grumbled.

Murphy put his hand up to stop him. "Alright, Alright, I'll put the branding back till the weekend. How much for that?"

"Fifteen cents."

Murphy raised his brows. "Fifteen?"

"Yeah, that's what it costs. You wanna take it to Ravensfield, be my guest."

"But that's a whole day in the saddle."

"Then I'll do it for ya, but my charge is fifteen cents."

"Okay, I have no choice. You're the only smithy in Crescent Valley."

Mitch turned his hand up and held it out to the man. Murphy frowned, growled, thrust his hand in his pocket, pulled out a few coins, and dropped them into the outstretched hand. Mitchell nodded, lifted the long-handled brand over his shoulder, and turned to hobble back to his forge.

Murphy screwed up his face at the retreating man. "Good day to you too." He shook his head and walked away.

Mitchell heard the sarcastic response and shook his head slightly. He shoved the coins in his pocket, leaned the brand against the wall in his workshop, and regained his spot at the forge.

*   *   *   *

Miranda Jones walked out of the bank; she put one hand on her back and rubbed her stomach with the other. She took a seat on the bench out front to wait, pulling her shawl around her shoulders. She was due in a month, and it was getting harder to be on her feet for a long time.

"Morning, Mrs. Jones." Sheriff Connor tipped his hat to her as he walked past.

Miranda smiled and nodded to him. "Morning, Sheriff, lovely day, isn't it?"

The sheriff paused and looked up at her. "Yes, it's pleasant now; I prefer this time of year to the heat of summer."

"Me too. Spring in Montana is so beautiful."

"Sure is, Ma'am. I best get going."

"Good day, Sheriff." She nodded to him, pushed her bonnet back off her head and let the sun shine on her golden hair. Her husband would be some time in the bank, but she was happy to wait in the warm sun. She cast her eyes to the edge of town and sighed as they fell on Mitchell Sullivan leaning over the rail outside his

43

workshop, talking to Mr. Murphy. She frowned as she watched him thrust the brand over his shoulder and hobble away. Guilt washed over her, and she sighed.

"I wonder if he'll ever forgive me." She shook her head.

"Why are you worried about him forgiving you?" Charlie stepped out of the bank. "He's a bitter old recluse."

Miranda took her husband's hand and stood up. "Probably because of what happened to him and then what I did." She closed her eyes and sighed.

Charlie screwed up his nose, lifted Miranda's basket, gave her his arm, and led her down the street towards the café. "It's not your problem; he lost you to a better man."

Miranda gave him a slight nod and bit her lips together. He never caught the small gesture, and it was fortunate he couldn't hear her thoughts. *I'm not entirely sure about that.* Charlie had both legs intact and took care of her, but she wouldn't call what they had "love" exactly. There wasn't a day that went by that she didn't live with some regret for turning her back on Mitch.

The blacksmith was a gentle man, if not somewhat shy sometimes. She remembered when he'd proposed to her a few months before the accident. They'd been so much in love.

She sighed and shook her head.

"What is it? You aren't still feeling sorry for him, are you?"

"In some ways."

"Why? He isn't your problem anymore. You're my wife and having my child."

And it had better be a boy or so help it. She cringed at the thought; the man was insistent he only wanted sons to help on the farm. "I know; I chose you, remember," she murmured. Miranda often wondered what might have been and lived with guilt and shame that she'd rejected the man she loved just because he'd lost his leg. He'd become aloof and reclusive since and it was her fault. She sighed again and then dragged her mind back to Charlie.

"Will you stay and have coffee with us today?"

"Your brother be there?"

"No, he's working; you know that the store doesn't run itself."

Charlie shrugged and screwed up his face. "You want me to sit around with a bunch of ladies talking 'bout lace and flowers?"

Miranda grimaced. "Only two ladies; we don't talk about lace and flowers."

"Still, I'll give it a miss if you don't mind. Why do you keep asking me to come anyway?"

"Because I thought you might like to spend time with your wife."

He looked at her as they entered the café. "Why?"

She sighed loudly. "No reason."

He seated her opposite her sister-in-law Clara. "Be back for you in an hour."

"Thank you." She smiled kindly.

With barely a nod, he turned and walked away.

Clara shook her head and frowned. "That man doesn't appreciate you nearly enough."

"He means well; he's just not a romantic kind. He treats me okay," Miranda insisted. But Clara couldn't see the bruises that were hidden under her dress. He didn't hit her often, just enough to keep her compliant. Now that she was pregnant, she didn't want to upset the apple cart.

Clara put her hand on her sister-in-law's arm. "You deserve far more than 'okay,' Mandy; you deserve to be treated like a princess, especially now that you're expecting."

Miranda shrugged. Clara was the only person who ever called her Mandy. It didn't bother her. They'd been friends ever since she and her brother had moved to the Montana territory with their father to open the mercantile. She chuckled as she remembered Clara holding her hand on the first day of school as an eight-year-old, helping her find her way and meet the other girls. She was grateful for Clara's much more outgoing nature. She was bubbly and fun, and she couldn't blame her brother for falling hopelessly in love with the pretty brunette.

"I'm okay, Clara; at least he doesn't hit me. I'm glad about that." Her lip trembled, and she looked down, hoping Clara couldn't tell she was lying.

Clara grimaced. She had her suspicions that wasn't the complete truth. "It's sad to think you aren't happy in your marriage."

"What makes you think we aren't happy?"

Clara tipped her head to the side and raised her brows. "Are you?"

Miranda sighed. "It's been better since I found out about the baby. It took over a year, and he was starting to think I was barren. I sure hope for his sake this baby is a boy."

Clara nodded to Alice as she placed their meals before them. They got the same thing every Wednesday when they met together. "He'll love the baby even if it turns out to be a girl."

"I'm not so sure. He's made it clear that girls are my business. Only sons are necessary for the farm work."

Clara frowned. "I couldn't imagine Mitchell ever saying something like that."

Miranda scowled at her. "You promised you wouldn't mention Mitchell to me."

"He's a part of your life, Mandy; you were going to be married."

"I know!" Miranda's lip quivered slightly. "I'm aware, thank you, but I don't need to be reminded."

"Okay. I'll let it go... for now." Clara shook her head. *He would have been a much better match, at least before he became so withdrawn. Mind you, with all the hurt he's faced, I'm not surprised he is that way. She really broke his heart.*

Seven

Mitchell extinguished the fire in his forge and cleaned up his yard. His leg was in agony, and he couldn't wait to get home to take off the prothesis and let his leg cool down. He stepped out the front gate and looked up in alarm as a wagon almost knocked him down. The man in the wagon swerved around him. "Get out of the way; you crippled fool."

Mitchell caught the eye of Charlie Jones and his wife as they drove past. He grimaced and sighed loudly. Seeing Miranda still made his heart ache. She was beautiful and sweet and far too good for that man. He couldn't help but think it should have been him, and his wife and child. He and Miranda had looked forward to having a family one day.

He ran his fingers through his greasy hair and hobbled towards his tiny cabin. "She made her choice; she rejected you. How can you still have feelings for her?" He sucked in a breath and forced the feelings down. It was wrong to hold a candle for another man's wife, but then she'd very nearly been his wife. It wasn't him that walked away.

"If it weren't for my leg." He sighed. Sometimes he wished he'd just died when those logs had rolled over him. Of course, the pain of his recovery had been excruciating, long, and tedious. It still gave him pain at times, but the pain of losing Miranda was even worse. That was over a year ago, and he still couldn't quite shake the 'what ifs' from his mind.

Mitchell opened the door to his cabin. It was a small two-room wooden house, sparsely furnished but clean. He walked in and closed the door, snatched his crutch from its spot, and slumped into his armchair. "Ohhhhh." He let out a loud groan. It was the first time he'd sat down all day. He bent down and rolled up his trouser leg. Unstrapping the cumbersome leg, he thrust it aside, pulled the bandage from his stump, and rubbed it. He reached down, untied the boot from his right leg, and took it off—such a relief.

He was made fun of for being a cripple by some of the same people who'd saved his life. It was hard to understand folks sometimes. One minute they rescued him and did everything they could to keep him alive, but now that he wasn't as fast as he used to be and was often wobbly on his prosthetic leg, they laughed at him. It was worse when he went out without the wooden limb, on his crutch, with his trouser leg pinned up. He'd grown used to the stares and scoffing.

After a time, Mitchell stood, took his crutch, and hobbled over to wash up at the basin by the back door. He prepared himself a basic supper of bread, jam, and cheese, trying desperately to keep his mind off Miranda and his pitiful life, but he couldn't. Seeing her on the wagon, in the lemon dress with the pretty grey shawl with yellow flowers stitched on it, made his heart ache. He'd given her the shawl for her eighteenth birthday.

Mitchell slumped down at his dining table and picked up his sandwich. "What did she ever see in him?" He knew. The man was able-bodied, strong, and one of the wealthiest farmers on the Montana plains. He could give her a life that Mitchell never could've.

"She's not even happy with him." He sighed. "He doesn't treat her right." He ran his fingers through his hair. "He's got a fortune; all I have is misfortune."

Mitchell wasn't destitute. He lived simply by choice, not by necessity, and didn't see the point of having a big house when he lived alone. He had everything he needed in his tiny cabin.

He had some inheritance from his late parents and had taken on his father's prosperous blacksmith business. He was comfortable but not nearly as wealthy as Charlie Jones.

He shrugged. "I thought that didn't matter to women. I thought she loved me for me; obviously, she didn't. I gotta find a way to get over her. She made her choice," he scolded himself and took a large bite of sandwich.

* * * *

Mitchell ran a hand over the twisted metal and smiled as he checked the paint work. He loved designing the decorative pieces, and for the most part, they sold well. He didn't have nearly as much time to be creative as he'd like; he still had to make a living. He placed the project aside and walked back out to his forge. He sighed loudly. "Curse these horseshoes." He picked one up with his tongs and thrust it in the flames until it glowed a deep red, pulled it out, laid it on his anvil, and began to knock it into shape around the horn, which made it so much easier to form the curve.

He paused mid-strike with the hammer in the air and listened. Nothing! He shrugged and hit the shoe again. He froze; there was definitely a strange noise. It sounded like a wounded animal. He put down the shoe, took off his gloves, and apron, and hobbled in the direction the sound came from. Walking around the back of the mercantile, he noticed a solitary figure clinging to the wall, clutching her abdomen and groaning.

"Miranda?" Mitchell hurried to her. There were bruises on her face, and her clothing was torn. Patches of blood seeped through her dress, and he gasped. "Miranda, what happened?"

She groaned loudly and reached a hand out to him. Her swollen and bloody lip trembled, and her eye was partially closed and red.

"Miranda." Mitchell's blood boiled. "Did he do this?" he spat.

"I..." She attempted to speak. "I... wouldn't cook for... him... I was... too sore."

"And he beat you?" Mitchell could barely get the horrifying words past his throat.

She merely nodded.

Mitchell exhaled loudly and growled; he ached for her. *I will kill him!* "Come on; I'll get you to the doc."

He carefully scooped her up in his arms. She groaned loudly and leaned her head and hands against his chest.

He wobbled a bit, but regained his balance and hurried toward the infirmary.

Archie was sweeping the steps when Mitchell strode past. "Mitch? Mir?" He dropped his broom and turned into the store. "Pa," he called and followed Mitchell towards the infirmary. He caught up with them just as Mitchell walked through the door.

"Doc." He hobbled in and placed Miranda on the bed.

Doctor Wells poked his head out his office door and gasped. "Mrs. Jones." He hurried over.

"I found her like this, Doc. I believe that man beat her," Mitch hissed through gritted teeth.

"Thank you. I'll check her out."

Brian and Archie walked to the waiting room with Mitchell. "Where'd you find her, Son?" Brian asked.

"Around the back of the mercantile. It seems she staggered all the way to town from the farm in that state." He clenched and unclenched his fists.

Brian gripped his shoulder. "Thanks for bringing her in. I'm glad you found her when you did. You go, we'll keep you up to date with...."

A loud cry cut through their conversation, and they hurried to the examination room. The doctor turned to them. "She's in labor."

"Ohhhh." Brian hurried to her side. "Darling." He stroked her brow.

"You all need to leave please." The nurse walked in and strapped on her apron.

"I'd like to stay with her if you don't mind. She ought to have someone with her." Brian looked at the nurse.

The doctor nodded, and he took his seat by her head.

Mitchell and Archie strode out into the waiting room. Mitchell paced back and forth, muttering under his breath.

Archie leaned against the wall and sighed loudly. He watched the agitated man. *He really loves her; why did she ever choose Charlie over him?* "I'm going to get Clara; she'll want to be here."

Mitchell nodded to him and took a seat, burying his head in his hands with his elbows on his knees. He prayed for the first time since Miranda had walked away from him. *God, please protect Miranda and the baby.*

Archie returned with Clara, and the three sat in silence, waiting. The cries from the room next door pierced their hearts. Close to an hour later, they heard the shrill cry of a newborn. All three released their breaths and gave each other tentative smiles.

It was some time before Brian walked out with the baby in his arms. Tears streamed down his cheeks. All three leaped up and walked to him. Brian passed the baby to Clara.

"Pa?" Archie placed his hand on his father's shoulder.

Brian took a deep breath and swiped at his eyes. "It's a girl; Miranda wants her to be called Tillie Clara."

"Ohhh. Hi Tillie." Clara cooed to the girl. Mitchell grinned.

"What is it, Pa?" Archie frowned. There was more than the joy of a baby in his tears.

"She..." Brian sighed loudly and stifled a sob. "She didn't... make it."

"What?" Mitchell and Archie exclaimed at the same time.

The doctor walked out then, a look of devastation on his face. "I believe the beating she received put her into shock and premature labor. The trauma and stress were too much for her. She whispered the name of the baby and then breathed her last. I did what I could to revive her." He let out a sob.

Mitchell gripped his shoulder. "You did what you could, Doc." He grimaced, clenched his jaw, and strode out the door, ignoring the pain in his leg.

Archie held Clara and the baby tightly.

"Clara, I think it's best you take the girl home, at least till we find out what Charlie wants." Brian grimaced.

Clara's lip trembled. "I'd be happy to. Mrs. Tanner can help me with feeding and care. Her Edward is nearly ten months old."

"Good idea, Darling." Archie smiled at her.

"Where do you think Mitchell went?" The doctor grimaced.

"I'd put money on him going to sort out Charlie. I know he still loves Miranda." Archie scratched his chin.

"Oh no. I'll get the sheriff; the last thing we need is Mitch taking the law into his own hands. Besides, this girl is gonna need her father, no matter who he is," Brian hissed through his teeth.

"Mandy told me he wasn't interested in girls, only wanted boys to help on the spread." Clara rocked the small girl gently.

"Oh no. Well, you two take her home and get her looked after. I'll get the sheriff and head out to the Jones ranch. Thank you, Doc."

"I'll take care of your daughter, Brian. Annie has gone to fetch the reverend."

The man nodded and hurried out.

The doctor turned to Clara and Archie. "Come into my office; I have some things you could use for the baby, including a bottle to feed her."

"Thank you." Clara's eyes filled with tears. She whispered to the little girl. "Tillie, your ma was my best friend. I loved her very much, and you're going to be loved too."

Eight

Brian and Sheriff Connor hastened the wagon. As they approached the farm; they heard yelling coming from the barn. Leaping off the wagon, they ran in.

Mitchell had Charlie pinned against the wall. He was black and blue and had blood streaming from a cut on his head. Mitch had his arm across the man's throat. "You think it okay to hit a woman? You coward."

Charlie gripped Mitchell's arm with both hands and tried to speak. "I'm... Ssss...sss...sorry..." he whimpered.

"I'll give you sorry." Mitch pulled his hand back and punched the man in the jaw again, thrusting his head back into the boards. Charlie slumped to the ground just as the sheriff strode in.

Charlie groaned, and Mitchell bent down to grab him again. Sheriff Connor walked towards them. "Sullivan, stop!"

"No, Sir. He needs a taste of his own medicine. It's only what he deserves." Mitch seethed, picked the man up again, and thrust him roughly against the wall. Charlie spat blood and a tooth at Mitch; his swollen tongue meant he couldn't speak.

"Mitch." Both older men approached and put their hands on his shoulders.

Mitchell turned and dropped Charlie to the ground. "Just let me kill 'im," he sneered.

"No, can't do that, Son; he's not worth you losing your life over." Brian gripped his shoulder.

"I don't care. I'm gonna kill 'im." Mitchell's face was red. "Like he killed Miranda."

"Come on, Sully; you need a night in the cells to calm down."

"You'd better lock me up, Sheriff, 'cause if you don't, I'm gonna come back here and finish what I started. He took her from me, and now she's dead, she's dead, you piece of filth," he spat at Charlie.

"Come on." The sheriff guided Mitch away. "Brian, hitch his wagon and take that cretin to the doc. Let him see what he did to his wife, and maybe the doctor will be kind enough to bandage his wounds."

"Just let him die," Mitch sneered as the sheriff walked him out.

"I wish I could, Sullivan, but unfortunately, the law is on his side. Your wife is your property; he wouldn't even get a smack on the hand."

Mitchell seethed. "That's so wrong; she didn't deserve that; she didn't deserve him." He growled and punched at the wagon box, leaning back against the side with his one good knee up, he broke down in sobs. "Miranda, I never stopped loving you."

"I'm sorry to have to lock you in there, Mitch; it's for the best till ya calm down."

"I understand." Mitch sat on the bed and leaned against the wall; he gritted his teeth. "You have my word that if you let me out of here, I will find him, and I will kill him." His dark eyes and furrowed brow assured the sheriff he was serious.

Sheriff Connor shook his head. "I know, and we can't have that, or it's you who'll end up in prison for life. It's not fair, and I'm sorry, but it is the law."

"You gonna press charges against me?" Mitchell was beyond caring; his soul utterly blackened. God had forsaken him.

"Nah, you've had enough to deal with, but I imagine Charlie will when he comes to."

Mitchell just shrugged. "I don't care. What he did, the filthy piece of garbage, he deserved it, and I would do it again if I just had the chance."

"Don't say that. I don't want to have to testify that you planned to kill him. You're just a hurting man right now, and ya didn't kill him. The most you could get right now would be a fighting charge, if he lives."

Mitch nodded and hung his head. He knew that if Charlie died, he'd be up for murder. And that usually meant hanging. He shrugged. "Probably better than this wretched life," he whispered.

*   *   *   *

Brian and Archie walked into the infirmary. The doctor met them at the door of the waiting room. "I'm not sure it's a good idea for you to come in."

"Is he awake?"

The doctor gripped Brian's shoulder. "Yes."

"Let me speak to him," Brian pleaded.

Doctor Wells raised his brows. "Just words." Brian and Archie nodded their agreement.

They walked in and took chairs by the man's bed. Charlie was sitting up. He sneered at them as they sat down. "What do you two want?"

"We want to talk to you." Brian was amazingly calm; his faith kept him steady.

"'Bout what?"

"My daughter."

"She's dead; what about her?"

Brian sucked in a deep breath and noticed Archie clench his fists. "Don't, Son," Brian whispered. "Clara and the baby need you."

Archie exhaled loudly and nodded.

"Yes, my baby," Charlie scoffed.

"You aren't getting her, Jones," Archie insisted.

Charlie shrugged. "Don't want a girl anyway; girls are useless."

"So, you'll sign over rights for her to Archie and Clara?" The doctor had already had this conversation with the man and had taken the liberty of getting the attorney to have the adoption papers ready.

"Whatever." Charlie shrugged.

The doctor hurried out and got the papers before Charlie changed his mind. But Charlie was eager to sign; he didn't need a baby cluttering his life.

Archie and Brian both signed as guardians. Both nodded to Charlie. "You did the right thing. Tillie will have a good life with Clara and Archie as her parents." Brian nodded gratefully to the man.

Charlie shrugged. "Don't much care; she's bout as useless to me as my dead wife. I should've known she wasn't strong enough."

"You killed her, Charlie." Archie was rapidly losing his cool.

"Just gave her a few knocks; she defied me; it's my right to insist she obey."

Archie inhaled and exhaled deeply; part of him wished Mitchell had finished the job.

"I wanna press charges against that brute, Sullivan. He came at me unprovoked; he's twice my size. It was an unfair fight." He exaggerated somewhat, Mitchell was strong, but Charlie was the taller man.

Brian squinted at Charlie. "And you were twice my daughter's size; that too was unfair, and she was pregnant."

Charlie shrugged. "So? My wife belongs to me; ain't no different to a horse."

Archie stood up, prepared to grab Charlie out of the bed. "Arch," Brian called. "That's not the way."

Charlie sneered. "Cowards."

"Charlie, I strongly suggest you leave town and never return." Brian exhaled, trying to quieten his own rising anger.

"Why should I? Ain't nothing you can do to me here. I got the law on my side."

The sheriff wandered in; he'd caught the tail end of the conversation. "I suggest you listen, Jones; you may have the law on your side, but I can make a pretty comprehensive case against you for animal abuse and mistreating your workers." It frustrated him no end that beating a horse was a worse crime than beating your pregnant wife.

"What are you saying, Sheriff?"

"I'm saying leave town, never set foot in Crescent Valley again. If you do, I'll let Sullivan finish what he started."

"I'm not scared of him," Charlie sneered.

"You should be, and I want seconds." Archie gritted his teeth. Brian raised his brows at his son.

The sheriff locked his eyes on Charlie. "If we see you in this town again, I got a list of charges as long as my arm; your men are all willing to testify against you, said you been mistreating them and the animals on your spread for years. You'll go down for life; maybe we'll even hang you in the middle of town for all to see."

"You wouldn't," Charlie scoffed.

The sheriff leaned in and scowled at him. "Try me." He turned to the doctor. "Is he well enough to leave?"

Doctor Wells nodded. He despised the vile man, but it wasn't up to him to choose who he did and didn't help.

"I'll escort you out of town today. We'll sell up your spread, and you forward me your new location when you get settled, and we'll send the money."

"How do I know you won't just take it for yourselves?" Charlie glared at the sheriff.

"We ain't interested in your blood money, Jones. Now do we have a deal?"

"Yeah." He shrugged.

"I mean it; you step foot in this town again, and you'll hang for sure." The sheriff helped the man from his bed and marched him away immediately with nothing but the clothes on his back.

Brian turned to the doctor. "Much obliged for you organizing the adoption."

"I needed to know he'd never come back and try to claim that little girl. She deserves a good family, not him."

"Should've been Mitch's girl." Archie shook his head. "I don't understand why Miranda chose Jones."

"Don't be too hard on her." The doctor gripped Archie's shoulder. "She's not the first woman to be lured away by money and charm. The thought of facing what Mitch was going through affected her more than she let on."

Both men nodded.

"How is Tillie doing?"

Archie smiled. "Clara's the doting ma. She's a natural. I'm pleased for her. When you told her she couldn't have children, it nearly broke her. But she's been so brave and strong."

"Because she had you supporting her." Brian nodded to his son.

"Yeah, but now the Lord has blessed us with a child. I'm sad it comes at my sister's expense, but He's taken a bad situation and brought good out of it."

"That's God's way, Son." Brian stood.

The doctor nodded. "I'll see you two at the funeral. Archie, I'll send the nurse by to check on the baby."

*   *   *   *

"Sullivan." Sheriff Connor unlocked the door to the cell.

Mitchell opened his eyes and sat up. "Yeah."

"You're free to go."

62

Mitchell raised his brows. "Jones?"

"Drove him out of town myself. He's signed over parental rights to Clara and Archie, and he's gone. I told him if he ever sets foot in this town, he'll be hanged for mistreating his animals and workers."

"But not Miranda?" Mitchell hissed.

The sheriff gripped his shoulder. "It's not fair; I know it's not, but I don't make up the law; I just keep it. And in the eyes of the law, you'd be the only one in the wrong."

Mitchell hung his head. "I hate him. If I see him again, I'll kill him."

"I know. But Mitchell, right or wrong, he's Tillie's father. I know you care about that little girl, and Archie may be the pa she grows up with, but she is still part Miranda and part Charlie. Do you want her growing up knowing you killed her birth father?" Sheriff Connor raised his brows.

Mitchell sighed loudly. "No. Of course not."

"I know you feel strongly about this, 'cause had it gone another way, it'd be your child and not his. But Miranda is gone now, and you must find a way to get over your anger, for her sake and Tillie's. When she grows up, you can tell her all about her ma. But you can't do that if you are so bound up with hate."

Mitchell sighed and nodded. "Yeah," was all he managed.

"I'm sorry, Sullivan. You're a good man and don't deserve the misfortune life has thrown at you."

Mitch shrugged. "Just unlucky, I guess."

"Things may change for you in the future. You're still a young man; you may find another young lady someday."

"I may be only twenty-three years old, but I feel about sixty some days." Mitchell shook his head.

"It's the heaviness in your soul." Brian walked in.

Mitch nodded.

"You need to turn to God, Mitch; He'll help you."

Mitchell shrugged again. "Not sure I believe in God; if He is there, He's forsaken me, heaped nothing but misfortune on me."

Brian nodded sadly; there was no way his words would get through, at least not now; he'd commit Mitch to prayer. Only God could bring redemption to his blackened soul, God, and the love of a good woman. He'd pray that for Mitch too.

Nine

Wallace and Lola Fletcher drove into Crescent Valley in the hot sun of July. "This is it, Lo, this is home."

"Praise God; I feel like we've been traveling for months."

Rueben and Marvin drove the second wagon up beside them. "We have, Ma; we left Missouri in May." Rueben chuckled. "With stops for a few weeks here and there."

Ten-year-old Dora poked her head out from the covered wagon behind her parents. "Are we here, Pa?"

"Sure are, Darling. According to our map, the spread's just outta town."

"Hello there, folks," a voice rang out.

"Hi, Reverend." Wallace Fletcher jumped off the wagon and helped his wife down. The weary woman shook out her skirts as children clambered down from both wagons.

The minister put his hand out to Wallace. "Reverend Cross, nice to meet you."

Several titters came from the children, and Mr. and Mrs. Fletcher grinned.

The reverend chuckled. "Yes, appropriate last name. I guess I couldn't be anything other than a reverend with a name like Cross."

"At least it'll be easy to remember." Mrs. Fletcher smiled.

"You folk new to town?" The fair-haired, gentle man enquired.

"Yes. I'm Wallace Fletcher. This here is my wife, Lola. We've taken over the Jones estate." A groan came from behind them. The reverend looked over to see a young woman with auburn hair leaning back against the wagon with her arms thrust across her chest. All heads turned to look at her, then turned back to the reverend.

"Don't mind her. She's just bitter 'cause she had to leave her friends in Missouri." Marvin grimaced.

The reverend chuckled. "Moving across the country can be tough." He looked back at Mr. Fletcher. "Are these all your children?"

"Yes." He touched the shoulder of the auburn-haired girl. "This ray of sunshine is my oldest, Isabella; she's just about eighteen, and our twins, Rueben, and Marvin. They're sixteen. Then, Max, he's fourteen, and Jacob is twelve. And this little princess...." He lay his hand on the blonde hair of the girl in front of him. "Is Miss Dora, and she's ten years old."

The reverend nodded. "Well, it's lovely to meet you. I hope you'll be at home here in Crescent Valley. You'll find many friendly folks here. Will we see you at church on Sunday?"

"Oh yes, Reverend, we're Christians; we'll be there." Mr. Fletcher grinned.

"That's great."

"Could you point us in the direction of the Jones estate?" Mr. Fletcher lifted the map and started to unroll it.

"You won't need that. Keep going on this road, and you'll come to a property in a few miles with big black gates. That's the estate. It's a little overrun; the last owner was a bit neglectful."

"That's okay; my boys and I are here to work hard. We plan to make a good go of it. We got the land for a good price."

"Well, you'll be most welcome here. These are hard-working folk." The reverend smiled kindly, nodded to them, and winked at Dora. "I'll leave you to it."

"Thank you, Reverend, we're much obliged." Mr. Fletcher nodded and turned to his wife as the man walked away. "Do you need to go to the store? Or shall we unpack, and we can come back in later?"

"No, let's just get unpacked."

"Alright. You kids want to ride or walk?"

"Ride," they all said unanimously.

Wallace chuckled. "Alright, Fletcher Family, mount up."

"I wanna drive this time," Max argued.

"Alright, Son, jump up there with the twins. Rueben, Marvin, let your brother drive."

"Yes, Pa," the older boys echoed.

Climbing on board, the family drove away.

* * * *

"Hello there, you folks new to town?" Brian greeted the Fletchers in the store.

"Yes, Sir, we're the Fletchers, I'm Wallace, and this is my wife, Lola."

"Well, welcome to Crescent Valley; I trust you've settled in well?"

"Yes, we've been here three days now, Mr....?"

"Gibson, I'm Brian Gibson; this is my son, Archie; we own the store together."

Archie stood up from bending over a produce bin. He stretched his back and nodded to the family. "Nice to meet you both. I'm sure we'll see you around." He resumed filling the bin with apples.

"Are you folk homesteaders?" Brian asked.

"Yes, but we've purchased an established block; it's a little run down, though; gonna take some work to make a viable farm."

"Which block?"

"We've bought the Jones farm. Do you know it?"

Archie groaned and shook his head, and Brian frowned. "Yes, we know it. My daughter was the former Mrs. Jones."

"Oh, I'm sorry." Wallace grimaced. "We were told she passed in childbirth."

Brian nodded. "Thank you. We hope you're happy there and make out better than they did."

"Thank you. And I really am sorry about your daughter."

"I appreciate that. I'll leave you to your shopping. Will you be needing an account?"

The man turned to his wife. "Lola, get what you need, Darling; I'll make arrangements with Mr. Gibson." She smiled and hurried off.

Brian opened the ledger and started a new page, writing 'Fletcher' at the top. "My terms are, you can purchase on credit, providing you pay each month; after that, I add a penny per day to the charge. I don't like having to do that, but I can't afford to maintain my shop if people don't pay."

"That's reasonable, Sir. I appreciate that. It'll be cash on the barrel for us most of the time. We aren't rich, but we do okay."

"I like that. We are fair-minded in this town and believe in treating others the same. If you're fair and treat people kindly, you'll be very welcome."

"We came here to make a living, Mr. Gibson, but we don't mean to trample on anyone else to do so. We believe the Good Book tells us to love ya neighbor, and we do our best to live that."

"That's good. So, are ya settled? Do ya need anything?"

"I was going to enquire about the smithy; I want some work done, just wondering if he's capable of fixing the rather elaborate gates on our place. I'd like the Jones crest removed and our name put on. It's a big job; I might have to send them to the city." Wallace screwed up his mouth.

Brian chuckled. "We have the best smithy in these parts right here in Crescent Valley. Name's Sullivan, just over yonder past the livery."

"What's this Sullivan like? You aren't the first person to mention his name to me in passing."

"Oh, what's been said about him?"

"I got told he was a bit reclusive, somewhat surly, not the most personable chap."

Brian suddenly found himself strangely defensive of Mitchell. "He's a young man, but he's faced a lot. He was supposed to be my son-in-law." Brian raised his brows and gave the man a sad smile. "But he lost his leg in an accident, and my daughter broke with him." He grimaced.

"Oh." Mr. Fletcher scratched his chin. "So, what's he like as a smithy? Is he up to the job? Those gates need a lot of work."

Brian chuckled. He caught his son's eye. Archie scoffed. "Rather somewhat, Mr. Fletcher. You can trust Mitchell Sullivan. Haven't yet seen a job he couldn't handle." He looked at his son, and Archie shrugged. That was true; Mitchell was a wonder with wood and metal.

Mr. Fletcher squinted, not understanding the joke. "Thank you, Gibson; I'll swing by and talk to him. Ahhh, here's Lola." He smiled at his wife approaching with her full basket.

"Will that be credit or cash today?" Brian pulled the pencil from behind his ear.

"Credit, thanks; we still haven't got ourselves settled; when we do, I'll go via the bank and get our finances sorted out."

"Very good." Brian wrote the items down, totaled the price, and handed Mr. Fletcher a small piece of paper with the cost.

Wallace perused it and nodded. "Excellent, very fair prices, as competitive as I've seen."

Brian nodded. "Ain't out to rip anyone off; provided people pay on time, we can keep our prices low."

"I understand. Good day, Mr. Gibson, and thank you for the advice."

"You're welcome. Good day." Brian nodded to the man and watched him walk out.

Archie placed the paper on the desk, with the inventory on it. "I'd say Mitch can handle those gates, given he's the one that built them in the first place." They both laughed outright.

* * * *

Mitchell nodded to the man. "Sure, I'll give 'em a look. You want me to come and check 'em out myself, or you gonna take them down and bring them here?"

"Well, if you wouldn't mind, Mr. Sullivan. I don't have my tools sorted out yet. Do you think you can manage the job? They are elaborate gates up at the old Jones homestead. Do you know them?" Mr. Fletcher squinted at Mitchell, attempting to size up the man.

"Yes, you could say that." Mitch grimaced as the memory of Jones came back to his mind. "I'll come round later this afternoon 'bout three; that suit you?"

"Certainly. If no one is home, just go ahead and take the gates down."

"I will." He sighed and remembered his manners. He plastered on a smile. "Thank you, Mr.....?"

"Oh, I apologize. The name is Fletcher, Wallace Fletcher."

Mitchell nodded, turned, and hobbled back to his forge. Most people wouldn't be able to tell Mitch had a wooden leg, except for his limp. He'd adjusted well to the contraption and could even ride a horse, provided he could get on it without toppling over.

Mitch smirked as he walked away. "Of course, I can handle the job; I built those gates." He bent over the forge to shape yet another horseshoe. He made at least forty per week; the farrier over at the livery needed a constant supply. "Be good to get the name Jones off those gates. Don't wanna see that again." He let out a guttural growl.

Ten

"Afternoon, Mitchell," Clara called as she walked past. "Headed out of town?"

He lifted his toolbox onto the back of his wagon. He took off his gloves and hurried over to them. "Afternoon, Mrs. Gibson. And how is Miss Tillie this morning?" He smiled without meaning to. Tillie was one of the few people that brought a twinkle to the gruff man's eye.

Clara lifted the little girl so he could see her face. "She's doing just fine. Would you like to hold her?"

Mitch bit his lip and gulped. "I ain't never held a baby before?"

"You'll be just fine; here." She handed him Tillie and showed him how to hold her. He lifted the little girl and exhaled a funny laugh as his arms felt the baby's warmth.

He looked down at her and wasn't prepared for the overwhelming emotion that swept over him. "She's something, Mrs. Gibson." He sniffed away the threatening tears.

He really has a tender heart under all that gruffness. I can't help but think this should have been his child. She smiled and put her hand on the little girl. "Yes, she is. She's growing like a weed. I'm having a hard time keeping her in clothing."

Instinctively he lifted the girl to his shoulder and rocked her gently, patting her back. "You been sewing her new things, I bet? Miranda told me you were good at sewing."

Clara smiled again. *He's a natural with that girl, and he doesn't even realize it. 'Lord, I pray you give this man a family someday. He deserves to have that kind of love in his life.'* She grimaced. "I would, but my machine is broken."

"Oh, what's wrong with it?" The little girl began to grizzle, and Mitch patted her back a few times and lay his stubbly chin against her soft blonde hair.

"The foot broke; it's a fiddly little thing. I'll have to wait till the next time Archie goes to Ravensfield to get a new one."

"I could look at it for ya?" Mitch offered; he cooed to the little girl and rocked her gently.

"Could you? Do you know much about sewing machines?"

He grimaced. "Yeah, my pa taught me; we fixed Ma's a few times. I was rebuilding one for Miranda; it was gonna be a wedding present."

"You're building a sewing machine?"

"Well, restoring is probably a better word, Ma's old one. Nah, I never finished it. It's just sitting over there under a canvas."

Clara followed his pointing finger and noticed the large item in the corner of the lean-to under a heavy canvas. "You never cease to amaze me with what you can do with metal and wood. I love the window boxes you put on our home with the metal embellishments."

He gave her a half smile. "Been working metal and wood since I was a sprig, here in my pa's shop."

"I remember. When Mandy and I were girls, we always used to see you there after school when we walked your sisters home."

"Yeah, the girls weren't much interested in me; I was just the annoying kid brother, I guess. So, I spent time with my pa."

"And he taught you well. I'm sorry you lost them both so young."

He shrugged. "I've been on my own with the shop since I was fourteen."

"I remember that too; you left school after your pa died and took over his shop. I'm sorry you never got to finish your studies."

Mitchell shrugged. "I got plenty; I get by more than well enough."

"Oh, I know, you're 'bout the smartest smithy I've ever known."

Mitchell grimaced. "Not sure 'bout that, Mrs. Gibson." He passed the baby back to her. "I should get to my job."

"Mitch. I wish you'd call me Clara. We were friends once." She cradled Tillie carefully again.

Mitchell nodded. "Yeah, I guess it's hard not to have you remind me of Miranda."

She nodded. "You love her still?"

Mitchell shrugged. "I guess I always will. Weren't me that walked away." He grimaced and lifted a sledgehammer on to the back of the wagon.

Clara moved Tillie to one arm and put her other hand on his arm. "For what it's worth, it never sat right with me what Mandy did to you. She was never happy with Charlie."

Mitch hung his arms over the side of the wagon and sighed. "I hate that she died unhappy." He closed his eyes.

"She would've been happy about Tillie."

He opened his eyes and nodded. "Yeah, she looks like her ma."

Clara nodded. "That's for sure."

"Yep, she's beautiful." Mitch touched the baby again. The clock on the bank struck three, and he gasped. "Oh, sorry, Clara, I gotta go."

"Sorry for holding you up."

"It was worth it. First time I ever held a baby." He managed a smile and climbed up on the wagon. He'd got adept at compensating for his wooden leg.

"You're a natural with her."

"I'll come by and look at your machine tomorrow." He nodded to her and clucked to the horse.

Clara stood and watched him go. "You're not nearly as surly and bitter as you make yourself out to be, Mitchell Sullivan, and if some young woman can break through the wall around your heart, she'll have a fierce love indeed. I'm sorry Mandy turned her back on that love." She smiled at the little girl. "Come on, Darling, shall we go visit Pa and Grandpa at the store?" She hurried away.

* * * *

"That baby sure did look like Miranda." Mitchell sighed as he drove away. "Same soft hair and she even has that tiny lump Miranda had on one eyelid. She was so self-conscious about that, even though most people didn't notice. Course, I thought it was beautiful." He spoke to the air. He sighed again, and as always, his mind ran away to what might have been.

He cringed as he drove up to the Fletcher place. That man's name was on those gates; he couldn't wait to get it off there and throw it in the fire. "Wish I could'a finished what I started." He grimaced.

Pulling up outside the gates, he leaped down, and looked toward the house. A young lady was lying on a chaise on the front porch with her nose in a book. She caught Mitchell's eye, and he tipped his hat to her as he carried his toolbox to the gates.

Isabella put the book down and wandered over to him. "What are ya doing?" She thrust her hands on her hips and pursed her lips.

"What does it look like?" He frowned. Forthright woman bothered him, and this one was all red hair and freckles. Pretty enough, he supposed, but not the gentle blonde beauty of Miranda. This girl had piercing blue eyes that seemed to look right through him.

"It looks like you're trying to steal my pa's gates."

"I ain't stealing them." Mitch scowled at her.

"Then what are you doing?"

He raised his brows. "Your father asked me to fix 'em."

"They sure need it. Broken down rusty things." She curled up her nose and put her hand out to touch one of the vertical twisted bars. "Still, I bet they were magnificent once. The man over at the store told my pa they were the nicest gates in the territory."

"That right?" Mitch frowned as he took his hammer and began hitting the stubborn pins from their slots; they were rusty and didn't want to slip out.

"That's what Mr. Gibson at the store said."

He ignored her and went right on hammering.

She tipped her head to the side and frowned. "You sure you know how to fix these? Maybe they ought to go back to the city to get fixed."

He grimaced internally. This woman was much too nosey and demanding for her own good. "I can fix them."

Issy raised her brows and thrust her arms across her chest, looking him up and down. "You look awful young for a smithy. How old are you?"

"What's it to you?"

She shrugged. "Just interested. I'm always interested in people."

"I'm twenty-four." He scowled. The first gate came loose with four solid hits with the hammer on each pin. He braced it against his good leg and hobbled back to the wagon carrying the cumbersome thing. He lay it on the back of the wagon and started work on the other one. Isabella followed him over.

"Only twenty-four? Our smithy back in Missouri was nearly seventy; I thought all blacksmiths were old."

Mitchell exhaled loudly, trying not to lose his cool. This job was worth a lot of money, and he didn't want to jeopardize it by telling this nosey redhead that he was too busy for her inane babbling. "I been doing it since I was a sprig with my pa."

"Do you work with him?"

"He's dead."

"I'm sorry, how'd he die?"

Mitchell stood up and glared at her, but there was no malice in her voice, she seemed genuinely interested, but her approach was somewhat unorthodox.

He sighed and resumed hammering at one peg that was being especially stubborn. He gritted his teeth and whacked it as hard as he could. That did the trick, but the whole gate came down on him. He lost his balance and fell to the ground.

Isabella burst out laughing as Mitchell staggered back to his feet, lifted the gate, and shuffled to the wagon. She was still laughing when he returned his hammer to his toolbox. "Ain't nothing funny," he growled.

She bit her lips tightly together to stop the mirth, but her eyes sparkled. "Sorry, I shouldn't laugh. But I've never seen a man fall over like that, your legs buckling under you."

He grimaced. *Blast this lousy leg.* He ignored her and climbed up into the wagon. He tipped his hat at her. "Good day, Miss Fletcher."

"Good day. Don't you wanna know my name?"

"Not really." He clucked to the horses and headed away. He rolled his eyes and shook his head.

"Well, that was rude." Isabella frowned and hurried back to the house.

* * * *

"The smithy came to get the gates today," Isabella announced over supper.

Brian chuckled at his daughter. "Yes, I can see that, they weren't here when I got home, and he said he would."

"He's a surly fellow." She frowned and shoveled a too-large bite of potato into her mouth.

"Mr. Gibson, over at the mercantile, told me Sullivan's had a hard life. Was supposed to be married to his daughter, but this here Jones fella we brought the farm off married her instead. Broke Sullivan's heart, he said."

Isabella frowned and tilted her head at her father. "Why'd she leave him? Mind you, as grumpy as he is, I can't see why she'd court him in the first place. Although he is very handsome under all that surliness."

Mr. Fletcher scowled at his forthright daughter. He never wanted to squash her vivacious personality, but sometimes he wished she'd curb her tongue a bit. "Mr. Gibson said he lost his leg in an accident, and she didn't want to be with him anymore."

"Looked like he had two legs to me." Issy frowned.

"He's got a prosthetic, wooden leg under his trousers. Sometimes he's a bit unstable on it, but Mr. Gibson said he gets around just fine, and apart from his limp, you'd never really know. Still runs his shop, even rides horses."

"Wow." Max took a noisy slurp of his water, causing his mother to scowl at him. "Sounds like he's a clever man."

"Well, I hope he's clever enough to fix those gates. If he can manage that job, I have other things that need fixing." Wallace sipped his coffee.

Isabella put her fork down and stared off into the distance.

Her father chuckled and put a hand on her arm. "You seem pensive, Issy."

"I was just thinking it was remarkable how he handled those gates if he's got just one leg. It explains why he toppled over."

"Toppled over?" Rueben furrowed his brows.

"Yeah, he hit the peg really hard from the bottom upwards, and it came loose, and the whole gate came up in his hands, and he lost his balance and fell backward. I thought it looked awful painful, but he got up and carried on. Must've been his wooden one."

"Most likely, Dear." Lola smacked Marvin's hand as he tried to fetch another potato with his fingers. "Use your fork."

The young man grinned at his mother, scooped up a potato with his fork, and plopped the whole thing in his mouth. Lola shook her head and chuckled at him.

Isabella frowned and ran her tongue over her lips as she often did when thinking.

"What is it?" Dora asked.

"I was just wondering why she'd break it off with him just 'cause he lost his leg. Seems to me a pretty silly reason to break with someone."

"Yeah, I agree. I'd never break with your pa just 'cause he lost a leg. More to a man than a leg." Lola squeezed her husband's arm.

He grinned and winked at his wife. "I'd say she didn't really love him."

"Why do you say that?" Jacob refilled his and Max's glasses from the pitcher in the middle of the table.

"Because, Son." Wallace gripped Lola's hand and lifted it to his lips. "When you love a person, it doesn't matter what they look like or if something happens to 'em to change who they are. You love them no matter what."

Lola leaned over and kissed his cheek. "That's right. I'd love you even if you had no teeth and a wooden eye or lost half your face in an explosion."

"Thank you, Darling. Same to you, you'll always be a ravishing beauty to me, no matter what."

She smiled at him.

"I could never break with someone for such a petty reason if I loved 'em." Isabella raised her brows determinedly.

"You broke with Chester Austin." Rueben chuckled.

Isabella gasped and whacked her brother. "I broke with him because he told Missy Archer I was ugly, and he was only courting me 'cause Pa has money."

"He was not good enough for you, Darling." Wallace winked at her.

"I know."

"Well, I sure hope someone marries you soon, get you out of the house." Rueben rolled his eyes.

Issy scowled at him. "I'll be out of your precious way soon enough. I got a job today."

All forks were laid down, and all eyes swung to her face. Her father's mouth dropped open. "You did?"

"Yes, don't look so shocked. I'm no pampered princess."

"I never said you were, Darling. Where will you be working?"

Jacob closed his eyes. "Please don't be at our school." He grimaced. She'd done some work at their school in Missouri and had thought she might like to be a teacher at one time but had changed her mind rapidly when she'd worked with the children.

"I'm gonna be working at the dress shop. Mrs. Delaney promised me twenty-five cents a week, to clean the shop, serve the customers and maybe even help with some of the sewing projects."

"That sounds like a good job for you. I know you like to sew." Lola gripped her daughter's hand briefly.

"Yeah, it's 'bout the only girly thing you do," Marvin teased. "The rest is all climbing trees and horse racing."

She scowled at him. "Well, it just so happens that I like sewing. Is that a bad thing?"

"Course not, Darling. Ignore your brother. I'm proud of you for getting a job. When do you start?" Wallace grimaced at his son.

"Monday."

"That's great." Wallace squeezed her arm. "I'll see to it; Pixie is shod for you, so she's ready for you to ride in and back each day. It's a wee bit far to walk."

"I'll take her to town tomorrow; see if I can't get that smithy to give her some shoes." She blushed without meaning to.

Rueben caught it. "Ohhhh, you think he's handsome, don't you."

"What if I do?" She shrugged. "What's it to you?"

"Are you gonna marry a blacksmith?" Dora asked.

Both parents raised their brows. "Getting a little ahead of yourself there, Darling." Wallace winked at his youngest.

"What if I did? What's wrong with marrying a blacksmith or a farmer, or anyone for that matter? What's his job got to do with anything?"

"Nothing at all, Dear." Lola smiled. "A man's worth is in his character, not in what he does for a job. It doesn't matter if he cleans drains or mucks out barns for a job; at least he has an honest job."

"I agree. I will pick who I marry for their character, not their job." And she meant it. If there was one thing Isabella hated, it was snobbery and judgment. She liked everyone equally, and there were few people she didn't get on with. "I'm not going to marry the smithy, but I sure will try to get him to be nicer. He was awfully rude." She frowned.

"He's a busy man, and you were likely talking his ear off as you do." Wallace chuckled.

"I'm just being friendly; everyone needs a friend, Pa, even a surly old smithy."

Wallace nodded. "Just finish your supper, Issy."

Eleven

"Hello." A familiar voice made Mitchell's head snap up. He cringed when he saw that red-haired woman, standing at the front of his workshop with a small brown pony on a lead rope.

With a grimace he turned back to his forge.

"I said, hello." Issy thrust her hands on her hips. "Are you gonna come and see to me?"

Mitchell closed his eyes and sighed. Putting his tools aside, he strode over, and folded his arms over his chest. "Hello."

"There, that wasn't so hard. You don't need to be rude to people, especially not to paying customers."

Mitchell raised his brows. "You're a customer?"

"Yes, I would like my horse shod, please."

"I ain't a farrier; try the livery." *Why won't this infuriating woman leave me alone?*

But the woman persisted. She tilted her head to the side. "You don't shoe horses?"

Mitchell frowned and shrugged. "I know how, but Mr. Tucker over at the livery usually does 'em."

"If you know how, then you can do mine."

"Why?"

"Because I want you to do it."

He raised his brows and growled internally. "Why me?"

She shrugged. "Because I don't know Mr. Tucker."

He scoffed. "You don't know me either."

She nodded. "That's true." She put her hand out to him. "I'm Isabella Kathleen Fletcher; pleased to meet you." She smiled, and her eyes twinkled.

Mitchell's heart flipped slightly, and he frowned. *What was that?* He groaned and slipped the glove off his right hand. "Mitchell Sullivan," he said gruffly and shook her hand. He was struck by the softness of her hand and noticed that the back of her hand and wrist were covered in thousands of freckles, just like the ones scattered across her cheeks. It was strangely endearing. He'd never met a person with so many freckles. *I wonder if those freckles go all the way up her arms.* That thought caught him completely off guard and he dropped her hand abruptly.

She smiled. "It's a pleasure to meet you, Mr. Sullivan. Is it just Mitchell, or do you have a second name?"

This woman never gives up! He exhaled loudly. "It's Mitchell Irwin Sullivan, but I don't like my second name much." He shrugged one shoulder.

"I know what you mean; I never did care for the name Kathleen. Everyone just calls me Issy. 'Cept Pa always called me Isabella Kathleen when I was bad as a girl."

Mitch couldn't help but smile. He nodded at her.

Issy tipped her head to the side and thrust her hands on her hips. "Well, are you gonna shoe my horse, or aren't ya?"

Mitch looked across at the row of tasks he had lined up. He didn't have time; and really wanted to say no. But heard himself say. "Sure." He frowned slightly, there was something oddly compelling about this young woman, and even though he found her irritating, he couldn't help but admire her forthrightness.

"Twenty-five cents per shoe." He threw out a figure that he knew was much more than it should be.

Issy grinned, pulled out her reticule, opened it, pulled out a silver dollar to passed it to him.

His eyes grew wide as he reached for it. "Don't see many of these around here."

"We had plenty back in Missouri."

"Keep your silver dollar, Miss; it's only fifty cents. I was just teasing you." He frowned again. *Teasing! When was the last time I teased someone?*

"That's okay; I want you to have it, truly."

He squinted at her. "I don't take charity. I'll get you some change."

She shrugged, and he opened the gate to let her in. She stood in the yard waiting as he walked into his shop, doing his utmost to minimize his limp. He was soon back out with the change and four small horseshoes. He grimaced. Shoeing horses wasn't exactly his favorite thing to do, although he and his father had always done their own horses.

With a loud sigh, Mitchell bent over to pick up the front hoof. As he set to work, Issy wandered around the yard. She ran her hands over the decorative sculptures and broken machinery she assumed he was fixing for people. There were some fascinating bits. *Where do these plant stands come from? I've never seen anything like this.* There were wagon wheels and bits of steel everywhere, even a broken potato masher. She chuckled.

Her eyes fell on a large object covered in canvas. She moved her hand to lift the canvas. "Don't touch that!" he growled.

"Why not?"

"'Cause it ain't none of your business. Stay away from it."

Issy rolled her eyes and walked back to Mitchell. He put down the hoof and reached for a nearby steel bucket, turned it upside down and threw a clean apron over it. "Here, sit down."

"Thank you." She smiled at him.

The way her freckles danced on her high cheekbones when she smiled, made him inhale sharply. It was then he noticed that she had a single freckle on her top lip, on the left-hand side. A fleeting image flashed in his mind of him running his finger over her soft lips and stopping at that freckle. He exhaled and shook his head.

"Are you okay?" Issy frowned in concern.

"Ah, yeah." He ran his arm over his forehead. "It's just really hot today."

"You're right. I do love Summertime in Montana, though. The air is so clear out here." She pushed her bonnet back off her head and let it fall down her back. The deep auburn of her tucked-up hair caught the sun, and Mitchell took a second glance at her; his cheeks warmed, and his heart sped up. He fixed his eyes on the hoof in front of him, concentrating with all his might on the rough file he dragged back and forth.

He took three deliberate deep breaths to calm himself. *What was that?*

Just as Issy pushed back her bonnet Clara stepped out of the mercantile. She flicked her eyes up and paused, noticing Mitchell with a young lady sitting in the midst of his yard. He was shoeing what she assumed was the young woman's horse.

She raised her brows and clapped as she noticed Mitch's double take at the girl. Clara put her head back into the mercantile and waved her husband out. "Look at this."

Archie frowned and followed her gesture. A slow smile crossed his face. The young woman was chattering a mile a minute to Mitch, and Archie couldn't help but notice the man look up at her several times.

He looked at his wife and frowned. "You're making too much of it. She's just a customer."

Clara tipped her head to the side. "Have you ever seen Mitch let anyone in for that long, let alone have them sit and talk to him while he works?"

Archie frowned. "No, he usually chases them away; he claims it's because he likes being alone."

"Well, he sure isn't alone right now. And look at her chattering away."

"That'll be driving him mad; he abhors mindless chatter."

"He's not frowning, Archie." Clara smiled.

Archie squinted and grinned. "No, he isn't. Do you think we're seeing the ice begin to melt?"

"I'm not sure; it's far too soon to think that. But she's the first girl he's ever let into his shop like that, and she is rather...."

"Rather what?"

"I don't know the word I'm looking for; it's different to beautiful; she doesn't have Mandy's soft, gentle beauty. Oh, what's the word? It's on the tip of my tongue."

Archie looked at the girl as she threw her head back in laughter about something. He watched as Mitch looked up at her, and a slight smile toyed with the man's lips. "The word you are looking for is striking. She's quite striking."

Clara grinned. "Striking! Yes, she is. Of course, I haven't seen her close up. Do you know who she is?"

Archie shrugged. "Not personally, but Mr. Fletcher said his daughter was a vivacious redhead; I imagine that's her."

"That would be a whole lot of personality for Mitchell to handle."

"Well, gentle and sweet didn't work out for him." Archie grimaced and immediately felt remorse for doubting his sister.

"How would you feel if Mitchell were to court someone?" Clara turned to look at her husband's face.

Archie shrugged and rubbed his chin. "Fine, I just want him to be happy. What my sister did to him was horrible. If his heart heals after that, I'll be happy for him."

"Well, I better go. I hope this works out for him."

"You're getting way ahead of yourself, Wife." But Archie's eyes held a twinkle of hope.

"Perhaps, but there's no harm in hoping. I can pray for them both. You don't happen to know her name?"

"Not that I can recall."

"Maybe I'll go and introduce myself." Clara winked at him.

Archie squinted at her. "No matchmaking, Mrs. Gibson; that's up to God."

"I wouldn't dream of it. I'll pray, and God can do the matchmaking."

He kissed his wife, bent to kiss Tillie's soft hair, and turned to walk back into the store, shaking his head.

Clara took her time wandering past, trying to appear nonchalant.

Just as Mitchell put down the last of Pixie's hooves, he noticed Clara, and nodded to her.

She stopped and waved. "Hello, Mitch."

"Hello." He walked over to the fence.

Issy leaped up from her seat; any chance to meet new people she took.

"Hello." Clara smiled at her.

"Hi." The girl's face lit up. Mitch's eyes flicked to her face and then back to Clara's.

"Who's your friend, Mitchell?"

Mitch's cheeks reddened, and he stammered somewhat. "Um... She's not... That is... she's a customer. Miss Fletcher, this is my friend, Mrs. Gibson."

"Please, call me Clara." Clara moved the baby into one arm to shake the girl's hand.

"Isabella Fletcher, but everyone just calls me Issy."

"Well, Issy, it's lovely to meet you. I hear your family has taken over the old Jones estate." A slight cloud washed over Clara's countenance as she thought of her dear friend.

"Yes, Pa 'n the boys are fixing it up. Mr. Sullivan is gonna fix our gates if he's able," she teased, flashing Mitch a wide smile.

He blushed again and shrugged. "Yeah, I reckon I can."

"What's your baby's name?" Issy changed the subject, and Mitchell was thankful; it'd give him a moment to control his churning thoughts.

"Tillie. She's actually the baby of my friend, Mrs. Jones, she passed. Clara's eyes flicked to Mitchell's. He closed his eyes, and a slight tremble ran through his body. Clara turned back to Issy. "When she passed, my husband and I adopted Tillie, seeing as my husband was Mandy's brother."

"I see. Well, she's a dear little girl." Issy grinned.

"You want to hold her?"

Issy's face lit up. "May I, I adore babies?"

Mitch's brows raised, and he tried to stifle a smile. He watched Issy lift the baby into her arms and coo to her. There was the freckle again. Another image flashed in his mind; it was Issy, with a small red-headed girl on her lap, sitting in the chair before the fireplace in the house across town that Mitch had built for Miranda. He shook his head slightly and dragged his mind back to reality.

"I better finish the horse. I have lots to do." He hurried back to the forge before Clara could comment.

She smiled; she'd noticed a brief shine to his eye and heard him exhale sharply as Issy picked up Tillie.

"I better be going too." Clara smiled at Issy. She glanced at Mitchell; his gaze was now fixed determinedly on the shoe as he hammered in the final nail.

"Thank you for letting me hold your baby. I know it's not usual to let a stranger hold your child."

"You're welcome, Miss Fletcher." Clara lifted the little girl into her arms. "Tillie loves to be held. She's a precious little soul."

"Yes, I can't wait to have children one day. Being a mother is about all I ever dreamed of."

Clara grinned as she noticed Mitchell gasp and drop the hammer. He quickly picked it up and returned to his job.

"It's truly rewarding." A slight sadness washed over Clara; if it weren't for Tillie, she might never have got to be a mother.

"Yes. Well, good day, Mrs. Gibson. Ahhh, Clara."

"Good day, Issy."

Clara hurried away, grinning to herself. "Tillie, I think we may have just witnessed the start of something special. Oh, I hope it works out for him. Mitch didn't deserve what Mandy did, and I just want him to be happy. A young woman with spunk like that could be just what he needs to bring him out of his shell. He'll be a wonderful husband and father one day, even if he doesn't realize it yet. We shall have to double our prayers." She chuckled and hurried back home to change and feed the baby.

Twelve

As Mitchell drove out to the Fletcher estate, he thought about Issy. He'd found her flashing into his thoughts lately. It was just because she was new to town and looked so different to the other women he knew. At least that's what he told himself. When he closed his eyes at night, he saw those freckles, and that small one on her lip that only appeared when she smiled broadly.

He shook his head. "Snap out of it, Mitchell. You hardly know this woman; besides, she's so talkative and... the most irritating woman you've ever met." He scowled but was strangely intrigued to realize he hadn't found her as annoying as he thought.

Is that why I waited till today to bring the gates out? Because it's Saturday, and I know Issy isn't working at the dress shop. Sure, it was more convenient; it gave the paint an extra day to harden properly, but he'd had them ready for a few days.

Still, he was slightly disappointed to see no one appeared to be home when he drove up. "Oh well, it's just as well. You can't afford to find a woman appealing. As soon as she finds out you're a cripple, she'll leave you anyway." He sighed loudly and woahed to Nickel and Dime, his quarterhorses. Climbing off the wagon, he went straight to work on the gates, determined to keep his mind off Issy. It didn't take long to hang the gates, although the job was rather fiddly. He had to prop the gates up on pieces of wood and slide them down over the new pegs that held the hinges in place.

At last, he closed the gates and stepped back to admire them. He nodded. They were even more beautiful now than when he'd first made them. That horrible 'Jones' was gone, and he'd taken great delight thrusting the letters into his forge. In its place was a large shield with a curly 'F' inside the shape of a rose, the vine of which curved out around the long bars of twisted iron. He'd painstakingly cut out each small leaf and twisted the steel to attach them to the vines. The effect was becoming. It had taken him more than a week of long hours to finish the job, but he declared it some of his finest work.

Subconsciously Mitchell rubbed at his aching leg as he hung the key on a string over the gate, mounted his wagon and drove back to town.

*　　*　　*　　*

"Pa, look!" Rueben stood in the wagon and pointed to the gates as they drove up. The entire family stretched their necks to admire them. Wallace's eyes widened, and his mouth fell open. Pulling the wagon to a stop he jumped down, and stood for a moment, staring at the gates. The children and their mother clambered down, and they walked around and inspected the large gates.

Marvin ran his hand over the 'F'. "Have you ever seen something like this, Pa?"

"Yes, in the manor houses in the East. This is amazing work, even better than what was here before."

"Do you suppose he sent them away to be fixed?" Rueben touched a small leaf and the twisted vine.

"Maybe, I'd be surprised if a country smithy could do this."

"Maybe he did, Pa." Issy stood beside her father. "I saw some of the sculptures in his workshop, and they were amazing, 'course, I have no way of knowing if he did 'em or he's just fixing them."

"I'm not sure, Darling." Wallace put his arm around her. "It's not usually in the range of a country smithy."

"He started working for his father when he was not yet at school. Made his first horseshoe completely by himself at six years old."

Lola noticed how her daughter's eyes lit up when she spoke of him. Issy flitted from crush to crush like a silly schoolgirl. Still, there was more behind that grin than usual.

"How do you know all that?" Rueben asked.

"I asked him, and he told me."

"When was that?" Wallace tilted his head at her.

She shrugged and dragged her hand across one horizontal bar. "When he shod Pixie for me."

Wallace squinted and gave his wife a knowing look. "He shod Pixie? I was told there was a farrier over at the livery that usually did that."

"Oh, there is, but I asked Mr. Sullivan to shoe Pixie, and he did." She shrugged again.

"I see." Mr. Wallace stroked his chin. *Poor Chap, it seems you're her latest crush. Don't worry, it'll pass, and she'll move on to someone else.* He chuckled and reached for the large iron key hanging from the gate. "Dora, would you like to do the honors?"

The little girl let go of her mother's hand and hurried over to her father. He lifted her, and she slipped the key into the lock. "Turn it, Darling." It took both hands and a little help from her father to open the new lock. The gates swung open without a single squeak, and the family walked up the driveway to their home with Rueben leading the team.

"I'll have plenty of work for that smithy; if he did such a good job on these gates, imagine what he can do with a wagon box." Wallace glanced across at the broken wagon in front of his barn.

"We still don't know he did it; he's just as likely to have sent them away." Lola opened the door to the house.

"You may be right, my darling. We shall have to wait and see." He kissed her on the cheek and hurried to the barn to follow the boys with the team. He paused and turned to look at the gates. "That's beautiful work." He shook his head.

*   *   *   *

"Mitchell, are you there?"

Mitchell wandered out of his workshop towards the voice. "Hi, Clara." He raised his brows in question.

"Hi, I just came by to thank you for fixing my sewing machine. It works better than ever."

Mitchell shrugged. "It's what I do."

She put a hand on his arm. "No, you're exceptional, the work you do, all these amazing designs, fixing sewing machines, your work with wood. You're really talented."

Shuffling back and forth on his feet, Mitchell lowered his head and gave her a shy smile. "I'm not sure about that; I just understand wood and metal."

Clara nodded. "I wanted to come by and say thank you. How much do I owe you for that job?"

Mitch snapped his head up and fixed his eyes on hers. "No charge, Clara; I was happy to do it."

"Oh, Mitchell, I must pay you something. You came after hours; you used your own oil and parts you had around. It must have cost you something?"

He cleared his throat. "I wouldn't hear of it. You and Archie are as close to family as I got." His voice was low and emotion-laden.

"Well, at least let us treat you to supper. I'm sure Tillie would love to see her Uncle Mitch."

A smile toyed with his face, and his eyes lit up. "Uncle?"

Clara squeezed his arm again. "You're as close to an uncle as she could have. So why not be Uncle Mitch? You loved Tillie's mother more than anyone else. She'll need you to tell her about Miranda when she grows up."

Clara graciously tried not to notice the slight quiver to his lips. Mitchell merely nodded and swiped his sleeve across his nose, disguising a sniff. "Sure, I'll come. Tell me when."

"Excellent, or better still, let us take you to the café; Tina does a roast dinner with all the trimmings. Would you like that?"

"Sure." He tried to sound nonchalant. "Beats my jam and cheese sandwiches, I guess."

"Great, I'll have Archie come by and tell you what day."

"Much obliged. I'm glad your sewing machine is working; now you can make some new clothes for Tillie." He grinned without meaning to. "She sure is growing. Where is she today?"

"She's sleeping; Mrs. Tanner is watching her. I just stepped out to see you, and I have to run to the store to gather a few things."

Mitchell nodded, tipped his hat to Clara and wandered back to his forge. He added more wood to the fire and rubbed his leg sub-consciously, stopping abruptly to pivot around when a voice called. "Morning."

Mitchell held back a groan; he never seemed to get started on a project before all the interruptions began. He wandered over to the fence. "Mr. Fletcher." He raised his brows. "Everything okay with the gates?"

"More than okay. They look great. And you got them done quickly; did you send them to Ravensfield?"

Mitchell frowned. "What for?" He folded his arms over his chest.

"Well, repairs and painting."

The smithy's brows furrowed, and he pursed his lips. "Why would I do that?"

"Well... I don't know... You're a country smithy; those gates are very decorative, like the ones on manor houses back East. I just assumed they'd be beyond your skill to repair with a small shop like yours." He waved his arm around his yard and workshop.

Mitchell frowned and scratched his stubbly chin. "Why would they be hard to repair? If I can make 'em in the first place, surely, I can repair 'em."

Mr. Fletcher's brows flew up, and his mouth gaped open. "You... You made those... but..." He nodded and grinned. "You're mighty talented, Mr. Sullivan."

"That seems to be the consensus," Mitch muttered under his breath and chuckled internally.

"What else can you do?"

Mitchell shrugged a shoulder. "Most anything with wood and metal. You wanna see the projects I'm working on?"

"I'd love to. I'm looking for some decorative pieces for the house."

"Come on, then." Mitch unlatched the gate and led the man into his workshop. He stroked his chin while he walked, and tried to minimize the limp. He really didn't have time for these endless interruptions, but for a customer who'd been as generous as Mr. Fletcher, he'd make an exception.

Wallace followed Mitchell into the covered lean-to first; several projects and items for sale sat on rough shelves or canvas on the ground.

"This is good work." Wallace ran his hand over a smooth shelf held up by elaborate curly brackets attached to the wall.

"My own design." Mitchell shrugged.

Mr. Fletcher looked at him and shook his head. "Where'd you learn to do this?"

Mitchell shrugged. "Just learned, some from my pa, the rest I just worked out. Been running this place on my own since I was fourteen." He wasn't bragging, just stating facts.

"Well, I'm very impressed."

"There's more inside."

"Show me."

Mitch nodded and led the man into the area he called his 'shop.' On one side were workbenches, toolboxes, raw steel, and wood waiting to be turned into a masterpiece.

Long shelves ran the length of the shop, full of small items he'd created. On the floor in front were two long tables with the projects he was currently working on.

Mr. Fletcher picked up a steel weathervane and ran his hand over the rooster on top.

"This is good work. And all these smaller pieces. You did these?" He gestured to tin plates, small ornaments, animals, cutlery, and even some small items of jewelry.

"Most of 'em. Some I just repair." Mitch shrugged.

"Well, I'll have some work for you. Mr. Sullivan. Are you a wheelwright?"

"Have been known to work with wheels."

"Got a broken wagon, needs a new wheel and the frame straightened. Also, two chairs got damaged on our trip, they need fixing and a few other household items. You're the best smithy I've ever known. The chaps in the city had a lot more space and equipment than you but couldn't turn out work like this."

Mitchell just shrugged. He'd never known any different.

"Say, I see some jewelry here. I've got an old cameo that belonged to my mother. It's damaged, and my wife was hoping we could give it to Issy for her eighteenth birthday next month. Any chance you could have a look at it?"

"Sure, I can't promise anything, but I'm willing to look at it. Happy to check out your other projects too. Want me to come by later today?"

"I'd like that, Mr. Sullivan. Does mid-day suit you? I have to get to cutting trees this afternoon."

Mitchell shuddered; the thought of felling trees still terrified him. "Sure, I'll swing by."

"And don't worry, Issy will be at work. I know she talked your ear off last time."

A slight tremor of disappointment shot through Mitchell. "That's fine," he murmured. *What was that?*

"Very well; I'll see you then."

"Good day, Mr. Fletcher."

* * * *

Mitchell sat in front of the fire in his cabin with the cameo in his large hands; the clasp on the back was broken entirely, and some of the ivory was chipped. The base needed repainting, and the woven gold around the edges had loops missing. He turned his mouth from side to side while he contemplated fixing it.

"It might take a trip to Ravensfield to gather some things unless I can get Archie to pick it up when he goes next week."

His mind turned from his plan to restore the delicate piece to its intended recipient. He'd been caught by surprise to discover he'd been disappointed Issy wasn't home when he'd been by that day to check on all the projects.

He shook his head, drawing those thoughts back in line. Mr. Fletcher had given him enough work to last several months; the man was generous and paid well, offering Mitchell five dollars more than the suggested price. "Couldn't be any more different from the man who'd lived there before." He'd taken great pleasure in seeing the restored gates without the name 'Jones' emblazoned on them. The Fletchers had tidied the place up so much in their first two weeks in town that he barely recognized it, which was a good thing. The estate only brought back bad memories.

Now when he thought about the Fletcher farm, new memories took over. Issy talking a mile a minute when he removed the gates. He frowned and shook his head as he thought about her incessant chatter. "That little lady sure has a lot to say." But strangely, he'd enjoyed it. There wasn't much chatter in his life. He lived alone in his quiet little cabin and hardly ventured to town.

Mitchell drew his thoughts back to the present, the following evening he'd be dining at the café with Archie and Clara; he grimaced and pushed himself out of the chair, placed the cameo down and hobbled over to his wardrobe. Taking out his one good shirt, he hung it up in the hope the wrinkles would be gone in time. He wasn't completely uncouth; he could dress up when he wanted to.

He'd not really been to town since Miranda had died, and he hadn't entered the house he had built for her since. It just sat there, unoccupied and unloved.

He stared into the flames, and his mind wandered. He'd always pictured himself carrying Miranda over the threshold, her shining blue eyes sparkling with joy, her arms around his neck, head on his shoulder.

Mitchell smiled sadly at the bittersweet image. He gasped as the image changed for just a second. The woman in his arms had red hair. "What is that?" He shook his head. "It's not possible you have feelings for Issy; you don't even know her very well, and she's about the most irritating woman you've ever met." He tried to convince himself. Yet the image hadn't been horrific. It'd been strangely compelling.

"You simply cannot allow yourself any of these pipe dreams, Sullivan. The minute she finds out about your wooden leg, she'll run away, just like Miranda." If a woman who'd loved him could do that, then how much more a woman he barely knew, no matter how intriguing he found her.

With a loud sigh, Mitchell threw a piece of wood on the fire. "You're better off alone." He mentally locked up the house across town and threw away the key. That dream was for men who weren't crippled.

Thirteen

A freak storm blew down from the north and brought with it three days of driving rain. Still, work didn't stop just because it was raining. Mitch strung a makeshift canvas tent over his forge and kept right on working. It was less than ideal and produced a lot of steam, but those horseshoes were not going to make themselves. He sighed. "I wish I had a better coat."

The one he wore stopped at the waist and barely kept him dry. Water ran down his neck and over his back. He wore as many layers underneath as he could, but still, he was soaked through before long. The other problem was his wooden leg. Water got between the leg and his stump and made it rub something awful... He grimaced, rubbed his leg and turned to pick up another horseshoe.

"It's really coming down today." Issy had to speak loudly to be heard over the rain. She stood under the wide awning and sipped her coffee.

"Yes." Mrs. Delaney pulled her shawl tighter around her. "I'm going back in. You take your time and enjoy your coffee, Dear. You're doing a good job and deserve a wee break."

"Thank you, Mrs. Delaney. It's just nice to enjoy the outdoors, and I love rain."

"Very good." Mrs. Delaney squeezed her arm, nodded, and hurried back inside. Issy smiled as she watched the woman go. She'd been working in the dress shop for two weeks and thoroughly enjoyed it. She couldn't explain why she loved sewing. She snubbed her nose at most things considered 'girly,' but she'd always loved sewing.

A benefit of working for Mrs. Delaney was that the older woman let her borrow the sewing machine in her spare time. Issy frowned. "I wish we didn't have to leave our sewing machine back in Missouri. I know it wouldn't fit, but I miss it."

She sat down at the small table and chair under the awning and peered through the rain. Not many people were out and about. A few huddled under awnings or held slickers above their heads and ran to their destination.

Issy looked down the street and grimaced. Mr. Sullivan was working out in the rain. She could tell even from a distance he was soaked to the bone. His coat was short, and the makeshift canopy did little to stop the rain. She grinned as an idea struck her mind. Quickly draining her cup, she hurried inside to discuss the possibility with her boss.

* * * *

"Good evening, Mitch." Archie stood to shake his friend's hand.

Mitchell nodded, shook Archie's hand, smiled at Clara, and sat opposite her. He looked across at the small girl in her basket on the spare chair. He reached out and wriggled the little fingers. "She's really growing." His eyes sparkled.

"Yes, she's almost six months old."

Mitch's mouth dropped open. "Six months! That time has flown."

"Yes. It's hard to believe Mandy has been gone for six months. I miss her." Clara grimaced.

Mitchell nodded his head and sighed. Clara gave him a sad smile and gripped his hand. "I'm sorry."

"Not your fault." Mitch shrugged.

"I hear you did a good job of the gates at the Fletcher estate." Archie sat down with three cups of coffee, slid them across the table to the two others then picked up his own.

"They seem happy." Mitch shrugged again and slurped at his coffee.

"A great deal more than happy. Mr. Fletcher was in the store yesterday and raved about your work. He was shocked to find out you'd made those gates yourself."

"I guess I don't look like much, and they probably don't expect me to be able to do that. I guess I don't speak too well either." Mitch gave Archie a wry smile.

Clara frowned. "Don't put yourself down, Mitch; you're a good man, smart, and brilliant at what you do. I won't hear anything to the contrary. I know Miranda caused you to doubt yourself, and I'll always be cross at her for that." She put her hand on his arm. "But don't shut away your heart completely. There is a family in your future; I'm sure of it. I know under all that gruffness, there's a kind-hearted and gentle man. I see it whenever you hold Tillie. And don't try to tell me it's just because she reminds you of Mandy."

Mitch shrugged and ran his fingers through his hair. "I dunno. If the woman I loved could reject me because of my leg, then how can I expect anyone else to love me? Maybe I'm just better off alone...." His voice petered out as the Fletcher family entered the room. Mr. Fletcher looked over and gave them a nod. Mrs. Fletcher smiled. Issy grinned and hurried over to them. "Hi, Mr. Sullivan, Mr. and Mrs. Gibson."

Clara observed Mitch watching her face. She noticed the slightest sparkle in his eye.

"Hello, Miss Fletcher." Clara turned to her. "How is work going?"

Issy plonked herself down on a chair to chat.

Bold. Mitch squinted at her, but observed her face, longing to see that freckle on her lip.

"I love it." Her face lit up. "It's so good to be able to sew again. I've always loved sewing."

"That's great. I love to sew too." Clara smiled. Tillie began to grizzle, so she picked her up and rocked her.

Issy put her hands out to her. "May I?"

"Sure." Clara grinned and passed her over. Issy was the most forthright woman she'd ever met.

"Ohhhh, so lovely." Issy rocked the grizzly girl, patting her back to sooth her.

"You're good with babies, Miss Fletcher." Archie smiled.

"Oh, I've always loved babies. Everyone is so surprised that I like sewing and babies, but I'm much more traditional than people think. Just 'cause I like to talk a lot and do boyish things, doesn't mean I'm not a woman." She blushed. "Although I'm not the best cook, Ma's trying to teach me, but I just can't seem to pick it up." She shrugged and rocked the baby. "I'll get there in time to get married one day, I suppose." She rolled her eyes and grimaced. "If anyone will ever have me. Pa says I don't stop talking long enough for a man to ask me."

Clara and Archie chuckled. Mitchell remained silent, enjoying listening to the conversation.

"I love this little dress you have her in, Mrs. Gibson. The pale green is so beautiful."

"Thank you. I made it a few days ago, thanks to Mitchell, who fixed my sewing machine."

Mitch grimaced. He didn't want the praise.

Issy's eyes flicked to him as she passed the baby back to Clara. "You can fix sewing machines? I wish I'd known you back in Missouri; my machine kept breaking." She sighed. "'Course we had to leave it behind, we could only bring with us what fitted in two wagons, and with all my siblings, there was no room for the sewing machine." She glanced across at her family and chuckled. "I'd much rather leave the twins behind and bring my sewing machine."

Everyone at the table grinned. Issy threw her head back and laughed loudly; the freckle on her lip became visible, and Mitchell hid his grin by slurping at his coffee.

"Issy, our meals are here," her father called.

"Oh." She jumped up. "I gotta go. Enjoy your meals."

"We will, thank you," Clara said to her hastily retreating frame.

Archie shook his head and chuckled. "She has a lot of personality."

Mitchell stared intently at his cup.

"I like her." Clara grinned and placed Tillie back in her basket. "She's so joyful and enthusiastic. What do you think, Mitch?" She raised her brows knowingly.

Mitch looked up and shrugged. "I dunno, she's alright, I guess. Sure does talk a lot." But he couldn't keep the blush from his cheeks. He was grateful when Tabitha walked over and placed their meals before them, and he could change the subject.

While he ate his supper and listened to Clara and Archie speak, he stole a few sideways glances across at Issy. He couldn't believe she wasn't yet eighteen; she had so much spunk and personality. She was bright and articulate. It was ironic that the boisterous woman loved babies and sewing. Mitch's brows flew up, and a slight grin crossed his face as an idea sprung into his mind.

"What are you grinning at?" Archie shoveled a forkful of potato and meat into his mouth.

Mitch shrugged. "Just planning another project."

"Care to share?"

"Nah, just an idea at this stage."

"Okay, keep your secrets." Archie chuckled.

Mitchell shrugged again and placed his coffee cup down. "No secrets, just haven't figured out what I'm gonna do yet."

Clara nudged her husband, and they smiled to each other, noticing the twinkle in their friend's eye.

Fourteen

Mr. Fletcher turned the cameo over in his hands. "You've restored this beautifully. Issy's gonna love it. How did you fix the clip?"

"To be honest, I purchased a new one from Ravensfield." Mitch folded his arms over his chest.

"How much did that cost?"

"Don't worry; we'll stick with the one dollar. That covers it all."

"Don't be silly; I'm happy to pay what it's worth."

Mitch shrugged. "Nah, a dollar covers it."

"Okay, please yourself." Wallace wrapped the cameo back in the cloth and slipped it into his pocket. "I'm looking forward to Sunday now; that's Issy's actual birthday. She's a bit upset because she's missing her friends from Missouri."

Mitch shrugged again. "She'll be fine." He didn't know what else to say.

"Well, I gotta go and hide it before Issy gets home." Mr. Fletcher patted Mitchell on the back. "Another fine job, Mr. Sullivan; everything you touch turns to gold in your hands."

"I'm not sure about that," Mitchell mumbled.

"Haven't yet seen anything you can't do; you did a great job of my wagon." The older man gestured towards the wagon sitting next to the yard, with two large quarterhorses waiting patiently.

Mitch nodded; all this praise never sat well with him. He just tried to do his best with every job, even those infernal horseshoes.

Mr. Fletcher shook Mitchell's hand and turned to leave. Mitch headed back towards his forge. He stopped, pursed his lips, walked towards a large object in the corner and lifted the canvas off the top. He ran his hand over the polished wood, and a wry smile crossed his face.

* * * *

"The service was wonderful today." Issy hadn't stopped chattering since they left church, but then that was nothing unusual.

"It was kind of the Sunday school class to give you that gift for your birthday." Mr. Fletcher nodded to her.

Issy grinned and lifted the parcel. "I love this lace. I know Mrs. Delaney suggested it. She saw me admiring it when it came in last week. I can't wait to make something from it; I'll take it to work this week and see what I can create."

"Whatever you make will be lovely, Dear." Her mother grinned.

Issy touched the cameo at her neck. "I love my cameo; thank you, Pa."

"You're welcome, Darling; it belonged to my mother."

"You told me. I'm glad to have a piece of her; I never really got to know her."

"I know, you were only three when she died." Mr. Fletcher frowned as they turned the corner towards their home.

Issy nodded. They drove through the large open gates, and Mr. Fletcher grinned. "I still can't get over those gates; they're amazing. That man is talented."

"Pa. What's that?" Rueben stood up in the wagon and pointed to the house.

"What?" Mr. Fletcher flicked his eyes around and frowned.

"That crate outside our house?" The young man jumped down from the wagon and ran up the hill. "It's for Issy," he yelled.

"What?" Issy's mouth dropped open.

Mr. Fletcher pulled the wagon to a stop and leaped off. The children scrambled down over the side, and Wallace put a hand up to help his wife down. They hurried to the crate.

Issy lifted the tag; it was typed. She read aloud.

'Happy 18ᵗʰ Birthday, Isabella.'

She turned over the tag and frowned. "It doesn't say who it's from." She squinted at her parents. "Did you do this?"

"No, Issy, the cameo was your gift. I don't know who this is from." Her father creased his brow. She looked suspiciously from face to face, but everyone just shrugged.

"I wonder who it's from?" Issy raised her hands in the air and clapped. "Oh well, let's open it and find out what it is; it's awfully big."

Wallace fetched a crowbar off the back of the wagon; he put the teeth under the lid.

"Wait, Pa." Rueben grinned. "Let's all guess what it is."

"Why?" Issy frowned.

"Just for fun." Rueben tapped his chin. "I think it's...." He squinted and eyed the box up and down dramatically. "...a chest for your room."

He turned to look at his twin brother. Marvin bit his lip. "A new saddle?"

All eyes turned to Max. "Ummm, china?" He shrugged.

Jacob blurted out. "A doll."

Everyone chuckled, and his father scruffed his hair. "Would have to be a fairly big doll, Son." He grinned. "I think it's a big crate full of new dresses."

They all laughed. "Dora, what do you think?" Issy was enjoying the game.

"A horse?"

"Dora, I don't think anyone would put a horse in a box." Issy laughed.

"Maybe it's a toy horse?" The little girl shrugged.

Mr. Fletcher squeezed her shoulder.

"Ma?" Rueben turned to his mother.

Mrs. Fletcher thought for a moment. "An armoire, it's certainly big enough."

"Maybe." Issy chuckled.

"What do you think it is, Issy?" Max asked.

Issy screwed up her face and tapped her lips. "I think... it's... a big crate full of new books."

Everyone nodded. "Well, shall we find out?" Mr. Fletcher grinned at his children. "Let's say if anyone is correct, they don't have to do dishes for a week."

"Yeah," all voices said in unison.

Wallace pried open the lid, and they all peered in; the large object was wrapped in a soft cloth. He pulled down the sides, and Issy gasped; its shape was suspiciously familiar.

"Pull off the cloth, Darling; let's see what it is," Wallace encouraged her.

Issy swallowed, bit her lips together, and pulled off the cloth. Her face lit up, and her mouth dropped open. She thrust her hands over her mouth, and tears filled her eyes. "Ohhhhhh." She was much too overwhelmed to say anything else.

The family looked around at each other in stunned silence. Issy put her hand out and ran it over the smooth wood of the sewing machine. "This is so beautiful."

Mr. Fletcher touched her back. "I wonder where this has come from. It's nicely restored." A thought occurred to him, and he smiled wryly, but everyone was too busy admiring the machine to notice.

"Where did it come from?" Issy asked again.

"I don't know, Darling, but it's a most generous gift." Her mother slipped an arm around her. "I know how sad you were that we had to leave our machine behind. The Lord has brought you a new one."

"Yes." Her tears overflowed. "I can't believe it. My own sewing machine."

"It's an older model." Marvin touched the wheel on the side. "But someone has taken a lot of effort to restore it."

"Yes. Many of these parts look to be new." Rueben nodded.

"Well, let's not stand around worrying about where it came from or how it got here; let's just be grateful and get it inside."

"You're right, Ma." Issy grinned. "Thank you, Lord Jesus, for this gift."

"We'll take it in for you; where do you want it put?" her father asked.

"It could go in my room or the living room." Issy looked at her mother.

"I think your bedroom would be best, it won't clutter up the living room, and you can leave unfinished projects out without making a mess. Would I be able to use it from time to time?"

"Oh, of course, Ma." Issy gripped her mother's hand. "It's much too nice a gift not to share; you can too, Dora; I'll teach you."

Dora grinned and embraced her sister.

The boys worked with Wallace to carry the cumbersome machine into the house. As Wallace pulled it to the wall, he noticed a mark on the back of the wooden base of the machine—a burned-in brand 'S'. He raised his brows. He'd seen that brand before, on the back of the lock on the new gates, seared into the metal, and on many of the items in Mr. Sullivan's shop. He smiled but kept the information to himself. He wasn't sure why Mitchell had given Issy the machine, but there was a reason the man wanted to keep it to himself. *I'll honor that, if he wants to reveal himself, he will.*

* * * *

Mitchell walked to the front of his yard. Pulling off his gloves, he shoved them in his pockets. "Good day, Miss Fletcher." He observed her, the dress she wore made her eyes sparkle and it had a rather becoming lace collar. The cameo was pinned where the collar met at the top button. It gave her a sophisticated look and with her hair pinned up, she appeared older than her eighteen years. Mitchell was too enamored by her to notice the parcel under her arm.

"Hi, Mr. Sullivan." She smiled broadly. That freckle! Mitchell tried his utmost to keep the smile off his face. He couldn't explain why seeing it made his heart race slightly, he'd never paid any attention to freckles before. An image of him kissing her soft lips and touching that freckle flashed in his mind. Sucking in a breath he fought to bury that thought and searched his mind for something to say because the silence between them was deafening.

"I hear you had a birthday on Sunday; I trust it was a good day." He hoped he'd kept the tremble from his voice. *Pull yourself together, Sullivan. You know the consequences of falling for a woman.* He chastised himself, and concentrated on the chattering, trying to convince himself it was the most irritating thing he could imagine.

"Yes, I had a wonderful day; everyone was so nice. The people at church gave me this lace, so I made a collar from it. 'Course, I still have some left over, and I hope to make some things for Ma and Dora too." She ran her hand over it. "It's so lovely. Oh, and I got a sewing machine." She grinned at him and lifted her brows.

"A sewing machine?" Mitchell brushed his chin and tried to sound surprised.

"Yeah, it was just sitting outside our house when we got home in a big old crate. No one knows who it's from or how it got there."

"That's odd." Mitchell hoped his warming cheeks didn't give him away.

"It is, but Ma said I shouldn't question just be thankful to God that He provided it for me. It's so wonderful, you should see the machine it's been beautifully restored and polished. I've never seen the likes of it."

"Sounds nice," he muttered.

"Oh, it is. And I got this cameo, which is why I'm here; Pa told me you restored it for him. I'm ever so grateful to you, Mr. Sullivan; I love it very much. You're so clever with how you restore and fix things."

Mitch shrugged, his cheeks growing warmer. "Weren't nothing, just my job," he muttered.

"Well... I...." Issy became uncharacteristically shy. She shuffled her feet and bit her lip. "I um... I made you something."

Mitchell frowned. "What for?"

"To say thank you for the cameo."

"I just fixed it; it was a paid job; it's not me you should thank; your pa's the one that paid for it."

"But you worked hard; Pa said there were extra parts you refused to charge him for. You're a kind man, Mr. Sullivan; I don't know why you pretend to be grouchy."

"Who says I'm pretending." He thrust his arms over his chest.

Issy grinned and gripped his arm. "I do."

He gulped in a breath, and his heart sped up just a little bit.

"You can't fool me. Anyway, I made you something to say thank you." She handed the parcel to him.

He put his hands out instinctively. "You shouldn't have done that. It really wasn't necessary."

"Open it, please."

He nodded and gulped again. His heart sped up a little more, and his hands trembled as he pulled the ribbon. The paper fell away, and he lifted out a long coat. Issy took the paper, and he let the dark green serge fall to its full length; it was a long coat with a high collar. His mouth dropped, and he swallowed twice. He frowned and looked up at her. "Did you make this?"

She grinned. *That freckle again.* "Yes, on my new machine, it works like a charm, even on this thick fabric."

"I can't... I... I can't accept this, Miss Fletcher. It's too much." He tried to pass it back to her.

"Well, that's too bad. I made it just for you. 'Course, I didn't know your size, but you look to be about as big as my Pa, so I went by his size and measured it against his long coat the same. I think it came out well, even though I've never made one before. I saw you in the rain the other day, and you looked awful cold, even with your thick apron. I thought maybe you needed a new coat." She shrugged.

Mitchell stood dumbfounded, looking at the coat he held. Not even his mother had ever made him something so beautiful. He said nothing, just swallowed and tried to keep himself from trembling.

"Try it on, Mr. Sullivan; I wanna make sure it fits."

He continued staring, unable to respond.

"Go on." She grinned.

He nodded and thrust it around his shoulders, pulled it closed and did up the buttons.

Issy watched intently, with a wide grin on her face and that freckle calling to him. She clapped. "Oh good, it fits."

"It's very nice," was all he could manage to mumble. It was warm and lined with soft fabric. No one could ever be cold in that coat.

"I'm so pleased you like it. I was most grateful for the cameo, and I couldn't think of a way to repay you; then I remembered seeing you in the rain."

"There was no need…." His words failed.

Issy touched his arm and grinned at him. "You're most welcome, Mr. Sullivan; I like to use God's gifts to bless others; it's only right. I shouldn't keep it to myself. God gives us many blessings and talents, and we ought to use them for His Glory. Sewing's 'bout the only thing I'm good at, so I plan to use it to bless people however I can, especially since He was most generous to provide the sewing machine."

God's got nothing to do with it! Mitchell scowled. "Well, I'm not sure about God, but you're a generous person," he muttered.

"You don't believe in God?"

Mitch shrugged. "I believe He's there. I don't think He cares about me much, given me nothing but misfortune."

"My father told me about your fiancée leaving you. I'm so sorry, Mr. Sullivan, that's so horrible." She smiled kindly. "But God didn't do that to you. She did."

120

He grimaced. "Didn't stop it, though." His voice was gruff, and his brow deeply furrowed.

Issy gripped both his arms and looked into his eyes. "Mr. Sullivan, God doesn't stop the bad things happening to us; he just promises to walk with us through them. I had a beau once, and he turned out to be sneaky and unfaithful. He wanted things from me that I wasn't prepared to give him, so he chose someone else. I was hurt by that, but God showed me His loving grace and helped me to heal; He's blessed us so abundantly. All the good gifts we have are from Him.

"My parents lost three babies before they had me. They were devastated and thought they'd never be able to have a family. But they trusted in God, and they prayed every day that if they couldn't have their own children, He'd bring children into their lives that they could love. They took over the Sunday school class at church and loved the children fiercely. It was almost five years before Ma had me, safe and sound. They had five more children after me but lost two more since Dora. But they thank the Lord every day for His abundant blessings.

"Everyone has misfortune sometimes, Mr. Sullivan, but life isn't all bad; there are many blessings, too, and the misfortune, as you call it, helps us to be grateful for the good things. Put your trust in Christ; He wants to bless you more than you could ever imagine. That has nothing to do with things and everything to do with peace in your soul, if you seek God, you will find Him."

She grinned, and her eyes sparkled with such hope it made him gulp. He noticed the beautiful blue of her eyes and the sincerity on her face. He swallowed again.

"I..." He shrugged. "I'm not sure I'm ready to believe just yet," he mumbled. "Or at all. He hasn't given me much to be thankful for."

Issy smiled kindly at him. She squeezed his arm. "I'll be praying for you, Mr. Sullivan, that God will capture your heart; you deserve to be happy and at peace, not tormented in your soul as you seem to be. Oh, I hate to see people suffer when they needn't. Give your cares to God; He'll take them and help you carry them. He promises that." Issy removed her hand. "At least think on it."

Mitchell nodded, but that was all he could manage. His throat was tight, and he tried to keep the emotion off his face. *Why does she care so much about a man she hardly knows?*

The clock on the bank chimed, and Issy gasped. "Oh, I'm late; I really gotta go. Enjoy your coat, and thank you," she called as she ran, looking back over her shoulder. "I'll be praying." She turned her head, hoisted her skirts, and sprinted toward the dress shop.

Mitchell stood for a moment staring after her. His mind traveled to her words. Could he really find peace? "But all I've been given from God is misfortune." He grimaced as he hobbled back to his forge. His eyes fell to the workshop and all it contained. He looked across at his cabin; the land they were on was his. There was the house on the other side of town, the small nest egg he had in the bank.

"What's your point?" He scowled at God, who brought the blessings to his mind. "You took Miranda from me; you took my leg...."

A Bible verse his mother had told him a long time ago floated into his mind. *God works all things together for good for those who love him and are called according to his purpose.*

He scowled and thrust his hands on his hips. *What purpose? Am I called? How can all this possibly work for good, Miranda, my accident, how can that be good?* His eyes fell on Clara walking away from the store cradling Tillie. *Tillie is a good thing that came from a bad situation. And Clara gets to be a mother when she otherwise wouldn't. Is that what it means? It doesn't mean everything that happens to you is good, just that there's a purpose and often a good outcome from the situation.*

He frowned and screwed up his face. *What good can possibly come from losing my leg?* Two faces flashed before him, the two men he had pushed away when the logs started to roll. Two men who get to watch their families grow up because he was there. *Yeah, but two men also died.* He sighed loudly and unbuttoned the coat. *I don't understand. God, I want to believe in You; I know many who do. Issy said if I seek You, I'll find You. But where do I even start to seek?*

He sighed again, ran his fingers through his hair, and unbuttoned the coat, holding it up to admire it. Issy really was very talented. Only barely eighteen years old and so clever with fabric. Fabric in her hands, was like steel in his. *She said God gave her the talent. Is that true? God, did You give me this talent?* He shrugged finding no answers. All he knew for sure was that Isabella Fletcher had him more confused than ever. She sure had given him a lot to think about. He shook his head. "She really

123

is the most infuriating woman I've ever met...." He chuckled to himself. "And the most intriguing."

He hung the coat over the back of his chair and hobbled back out to his forge. A long day of bending horseshoes stretched before him. It came so naturally to him, he could make them with his eyes closed. While he worked, he chewed over Issy's words in his mind.

Fifteen

Clara looked up from her coffee cup and grinned. Mitch had his head on his hand, leaning on his elbow on the round café table. His forgotten cup of coffee grew cold beside him. She turned to look at Archie, and they grinned to each other. *Is that the face of a lovelorn man, or a man carrying a heavy burden, or perhaps both?* Clara reached over to touch his hand. "Everything okay? You seem so far away?"

Mitch smiled and sat up. "Yeah, I'm sorry, I was just thinking about something. Is... ahh, you said to me the other day."

"Oh?" She caught the slip of his tongue. *Did he mean to say, Isabella?* She squinted at him. "What did I say?"

"Something about all things working together for good." He shrugged.

"Yes, it says that in the Bible. I truly believe it. God can bring wonderful things from horrible situations."

He nodded. "Like Tillie."

Clara grinned and reached over to touch the little girl sleeping in Archie's arms. "Yes, that's a great example. I was heartbroken when the doctor told me I couldn't have children. I cried for two whole days."

Archie reached across and put a supportive hand on her arm.

Clara hung her head. "I thought Archie wouldn't want me anymore that I wasn't a real woman...."

Archie raised his brows and put the baby in her basket. He put an arm around his wife. "And I told her that couldn't be further from the truth. A woman isn't simply a bearer of offspring; she means so much more to me than that. Think about poor Miranda; that Jones chap just wanted a housekeeper and a woman to produce sons, he didn't value her, and it had nothing to do with childbirth.

"I would love Clara no matter what. If I had known before we married...." He turned to look her in the eye, stroked her cheek, and smiled kindly. "...that you couldn't produce children. I would absolutely still have married you. I love you for you, for all you do for me, for what you bring to my life, joy, happiness, and blessing. You're so precious to me, just the way you are. And I would rather be childless all my days than not have you in my life."

Clara smiled and wiped away a tear. "Thank you, Darling." She turned back to Mitch. "He told me all that, and we prayed together. We asked the Lord to give us people in our lives to love. We gave over the pain of our lack, and He gave us peace. We didn't know Tillie would come into our lives, and the circumstances were so sad, but Tillie doesn't have to grow up an orphan; she gets to have a family that loves her. You see, God doesn't take the bad things away. He just makes the best of our sin and shame."

Mitch ran his fingers through his hair and sighed. "I can see that in your life. It seems that everyone else has that happen, and I just have misfortune after misfortune added to me." He shrugged. "Maybe I'm one God has forsaken." He closed his eyes and sighed again. "Maybe I'm too broken after all."

"Mitchell Sullivan, that is the furthest from the truth. It's just you haven't put your life in His hands; when you do that, He opens your eyes and lets you see your circumstances clearly."

Mitch shrugged. "So, what good could possibly come from Miranda's death and losing my leg?"

"Oh, I don't know; perhaps God needed Miranda to walk out of your life so He could bring the woman He wants into your life. Perhaps you have some lessons He needs you to learn, or He just wants you to trust Him. We don't get to know all the answers. But we do get to rest in the knowledge that God has it all under control. There is so much freedom in that."

Mitchell shrugged. "I want to believe."

"What's stopping you?"

"I dunno really, just not certain I really can see the evidence of what you're saying. I see it in your life and Is... other's lives." He blushed; *why is she always on the tip of my tongue?* "But I can't see it in my own."

Clara was bursting to tell him that she was right in front of him, the greatest blessing he could ever imagine. The woman who would light up his life and complement him in ways Miranda never had; but he needed to work that out on his own. Matchmaking often just ended in hurt.

"If you seek Him, you WILL find Him, and He will open your eyes and show you." Clara squeezed his arm.

Mitch stroked his chin and nodded. "Yeah," was all he managed.

They sat in silence for a time, drinking their coffee. Mitch looked around at the busy café. So many people around had faced so much worse than he had. Mrs. Tanner sat across from him; the widow of one of the men who had died in the same accident that took his leg. He listened to her conversation as she sat with her daughter-in-law's baby in her arms.

"Oh, look at this blessed boy." Her face lit up in joy. "How the Lord has blessed us."

Blessed you? He took your husband. Mitch sighed; he struggled to understand all this. Issy had told him God had provided the sewing machine, but it had been his hands that had restored it. He that had used pulleys to hoist it on the wagon and sweated, trying to get it off. God had nothing to do with it. *Did He? Was it God that gave me the inclination to fix it for her? Why did I give it to her? I was restoring that for Miranda.* He sighed. He was more confused than ever.

Clara caught his grimace, she put her hand on his arm. "You'll work it out, Mitch. I'll pray for you. Why don't you come to the service on Sunday? It might give you some clarity."

He grimaced. "I don't think so. I ain't the church kind."

"What is the church kind?" Archie returned to the seat next to them with refilled coffee cups.

Mitch shrugged. "I dunno, someone good, like you?"

Archie's brows raised. "You think I'm good?"

"Yeah, you do everything right; that's why God gives you stuff. I'm too bad for God."

Archie chuckled. "You are not privy to the thoughts in my head or my actions. I'm not good. I'm a wretched sinner; I just happen to be saved by the grace of God. No more than that. If God truly gave me what I deserve...." He shuddered. "Perish the thought. Instead, Christ took it. He got punished, even to death, for all my filth, sin, and shame." Archie closed his eyes and shook his head. "I'm sorry He had to. But so grateful He did. There is no way I could ever be good enough to reach His standard without forgiveness because His standard is sinless perfection. There is not a human on this earth that could live up to that, save for Christ Himself.

"Instead, it's as if Christ and I swapped places somehow. I gave Him all my sin and evil thoughts, every disgusting thing I've ever done. Every lie, everything." He sighed, then his face lit up. "And in return, Christ gave me His righteousness. And now I can walk in His presence, and stand reassured that I am saved, that God sees me as He sees Christ. It's overwhelming." There was a slight tremble of emotion in Archie's voice.

Mitch screwed up his mouth and furrowed his brows. "And He stops you sinning going forward?"

Archie and Clara looked at each other and raised their brows. Turning back to Mitch, Archie continued, "I wish I could say that's true. I'm so ashamed to say, despite God redeeming me, I still sin; I still fail Him all the time."

Mitch frowned. "So, He has to save you again?"

"No, that's the wonderful thing about grace." Archie's face beamed. "When Christ forgave me, He took my sins, past, present, and future. I'll continue sinning till the day I die, because even though I'm saved, I'm still a flawed human capable of sin. But it's all covered by the grace of God, once and for all. Of course, that doesn't give us permission to sin; on the contrary, as the Apostle Paul says in Scripture; we don't want to sin; we are devastated when we do. We do the things we don't want to do, and the things we know we should do, we don't do, and yet, despite all that, I live in the assurance that God has redeemed me. And if I die, even while sinning, I will be in Glory with Christ when I open my eyes.

"You see, Mitch, it has absolutely nothing to do with me; not a soul on earth is too wretched for God because we all are, if that makes sense. One tiny little sin, even the seemingly most innocent of sins, is enough to condemn me to the abyss for the rest of eternity. But one act of love and redemption from Christ, and I don't have to live with the burden of that sin. He has His hand out to you. All you gotta do is accept it and follow Him; He'll do the rest. He'll do the changing of your heart. You'll change and grow and become more Christlike all your days. Of course, this side of Glory we'll never reach it. But what amazing freedom there is knowing I don't carry the guilt for my sin anymore."

Archie finished his rather lengthy speech and looked up at Mitch. He had his eyes closed, and his lips trembled.

Clara grinned at her husband. "That was so well said; you ought to have been a preacher."

"No, I'm just a storeman, but God can use even a lowly storeman, or a blacksmith or a mother, even a child, to touch the heart of others."

Mitch opened his eyes and nodded. He wasn't ready to let go of his hurt yet, but he certainly had a lot to think about.

Lord, if all this is really true, show Yourself to me. Show me that You are really there and that the things in my life can work out for good.

*　　*　　*　　*

All week Mitch turned the words over in his brain. His heart was all over the place, what with all that he'd been told about God and the growing feelings he had for Issy, although he hadn't let himself admit it yet. It was too risky to fall in love. Even if he were to win her heart, the moment she saw his leg, she'd run for the hills. He grimaced and shrugged as he stoked the fire in his forge. "I'm better off alone."

He picked up the iron bar and thrust it into the flames until it glowed red. Pulling it out again, he lay it on the round horn of the anvil and hit it, shaping it around the curve, thrust it back in the fire again and shaped it more. It was a long slow process, but he enjoyed watching it take shape. A cold wind blew, and Mitchell shivered. The days were certainly cooling down. It was mid-September, and no doubt they'd get snow soon. He wanted to complete some of these bigger items before he was driven indoors.

Putting down the tongs and steel, Mitch yanked off his thick gloves, pulled his coat around his shoulders, and did up two buttons. He grinned and stood up straight, brushed at the fabric, and shook his head.

"It's a beautiful coat."

He jumped in fright and turned to see Clara and Tillie standing at the fence.

"Sorry, I didn't mean to startle you. I just noticed your coat. Is it new?"

Mitchell nodded.

"Where did you get it from? I've not seen the likes of it."

He blushed and did his best to keep his voice nonchalant. "Miss Fletcher made it for me."

Clara's face lit up, and her mouth dropped. She grinned as Mitch reached for the squirming baby. "She made it for you? That's quite a gift."

"Yeah, I tried to refuse, but she insisted." He shrugged nonchalantly, hoping Clara couldn't see the heat rising in his cheeks.

Clara raised her brows and nodded. Mitchell was too busy cooing to Tillie to notice her expression.

"Did she say why?"

"She said it was to thank me for fixing up the cameo for her birthday. I'm not sure why; her father paid me for the job."

Clara's heart leaped for joy. *I know why, because she loves you, silly man. Oh, how wonderful that would be; a vivacious, young woman like Issy is just what he needs to light up his life.* With a colossal effort, she kept her thoughts from resonating on her face. She'd commit it to prayer. "It was very kind of her; countless hours would have gone into that coat."

"She got a new sewing machine for her birthday." His cheeks colored, and he took a deep breath. "And she was eager to try it out. It sounds like she made several things for people who needed them. One day, she saw me in the rain and noticed I needed a coat. I guess they're just

132

kind folks." He shrugged and hoped he sounded convincing enough.

Clara grinned, and then something occurred to her. *A new sewing machine?* She looked around his yard, she knew he'd started restoring a machine for Miranda, and he'd pointed it out to her. She looked around; a broken rocking horse and two wagon wheels sat in its place.

She tilted her head to the side and squinted at him. "You gave her Miranda's sewing machine, didn't you?"

Mitch bit his lip, and his cheeks reddened. He kept his eyes on the baby. "I uh... well uh... no... at least..." He stopped, looked up at her, and shrugged. "I had one, and she wanted one."

Clara's heart was singing. *He loves her!* She smiled at him, took Tillie from his arms, and laid her in the basket. "Why?"

"What do you mean?"

"Why did you give it to her?"

He shrugged. "She told me she'd had to leave hers behind. I had one that wasn't being used. It was her birthday...."

"That's a significant gift." She raised her brows and gave him a knowing grin.

He shrugged again and folded his arms over his rough leather apron. "I suppose so. It was just sitting around gathering dust, might as well do something with it."

"Does she know it's from you?"

"No, I just left it at their house when they were away."

Clara grinned.

"What?" He squinted at her.

"You are a tender-hearted man, Mitchell Sullivan."

"I'm not sure about that." He shuffled his feet.

"Is she special?" She raised her brows.

He grimaced. "Nah, I'm better off alone. She'll just leave me too, when she finds out about my leg."

Clara frowned. "Are you sure she doesn't know?"

"There's no way she could know. You can't tell by looking at me, apart from my limp can you?"

Clara looked down and shrugged. "I guess not, certainly not with that thick apron and wide trousers. What makes you so sure that if she did know, she'd leave?"

"The woman who loved me left me." He smirked.

Clara squeezed his arm sympathetically.

He grimaced. "Promise me you won't try to meddle. The last thing I want is for her to hate me. It's just better we stay as we are, and she doesn't know."

Clara nodded. "Are you sure that's what you want? You could find so much happiness and joy."

"No. It's not worth it. I can't go through that again. I'd rather be alone forever." His lips trembled, and he couldn't keep the tears from flooding his eyes. "It was more painful than my leg." He looked at his feet.

She squeezed his arm again. "Well, I promise not to say or do anything, but I will pray for you."

He nodded. "I gotta get back to work."

"Oh, I have that cheese grater I wanted you to fix."

She pulled the wrapped bundle from the basket and passed it to him. "No hurry, I have a spare."

"I'll get it done in a few days."

"I know you're busy, but I hope you'll come to the winter dance."

"I can't even walk straight. I certainly can't dance."

"Not everyone who goes dances; there is a meal too." She raised her brows and dared to ask. "You could ask Miss Fletcher to go with you?"

He closed his eyes. "Clara, I can't. Please leave it alone."

"Okay. I'll leave it alone. But for what it's worth, I think she's the perfect woman for you. I've never seen your eyes sparkle like they do when you talk about her. You never had that look when you were with Miranda."

He frowned. "Don't be silly; you do exaggerate."

She nodded and flashed him a grin. "Okay." She turned and walked away, praying silently. *Lord, these two are perfect for each other. May You work on both hearts....*

Sixteen

Mitchell stared at the ceiling in the almost complete darkness. It had to be the wee small hours of the morning. He'd got little sleep that night as his head spun. Clara and Archie's and even Issy's words turned over and over in his mind. Clara had suggested he had feelings for Issy. *Do I?* He certainly was attracted to her. He couldn't deny that. There was something so appealing about her. The freckles that sat on her cheeks looked like they were dancing when she laughed, and her cheeks bounced.

Her eyes were mesmerizing, a deep blue with flecks of darker shades of blue, and a defined blue ring around the edge. Then there was that freckle on her lip. He grinned. *Why does that intrigue me so much? It's just a freckle!* It was the way her face lit up when he saw it. He could only see it when she smiled broadly. He pictured her as he stared into the darkness. Yes, he was undoubtedly attracted to her. But did he have feelings for her?

He thought about the way she had talked incessantly while he'd removed the gates, and then in his yard when he shod her horse and several other encounters they'd had. Why did he give her the sewing machine? It was sentimental to him, it had been his mother's, long broken, but he'd been restoring it for Miranda.

He'd stopped a few weeks into their engagement for a reason he couldn't place, and it had remained under the canvas ever since. *Did I subconsciously know that it wasn't meant for her?* Issy loved to sew; she'd made him that coat, and it was the loveliest piece of clothing he'd ever owned. His mind drifted back over his courtship with Miranda. He couldn't recall a single thing she'd ever given him.

Miranda had never come to his workshop, not once. She didn't like to get dirty. Mitchell sighed, he knew he wasn't free of her. Even if he did have feelings for Issy, he could never do anything about it while he still loved Miranda. "Besides," he whispered into the darkness. "If she finds out about my leg, she'll run." He sighed loudly again and turned over onto his side.

Clara's words about God drifted into his mind, and Issy's. They'd all tried to tell him about the merits of following God. But he blamed God for all the misfortune in his life. It had all been going perfectly, in his control, until the accident that took his leg.

Since then, he'd had no control over his life. It spun whichever way it pleased, no matter what he did. He hadn't counted on losing his leg or the long, painful recovery; he hadn't counted on Miranda leaving him, marrying Jones, or dying in childbirth. He hadn't counted on living alone and meeting a woman who just left him feeling confused. He hadn't counted on the fear and inadequacy.

Mitchell sighed loudly and punched his pillow. "God, are You there? Show Yourself to me. Show me the way to go. I want the peace they have, the calmness amongst the chaos." Clara and Archie had been through so much pain, yet they had this peace about them. Issy had shared some of her family's pain, yet her face radiated joy.

He rolled over on his other side. "Seek Him, and you will find Him." Both Clara and Issy had said that to him. "But where do I start? How do I seek You, God? Where do I go to find You?" He spoke into the darkness, but no response came.

He sighed again. "Maybe I was right after all, and You have forsaken me." Closing his eyes tightly, he tried to silence all the swirling thoughts. At last, he fell into a fitful sleep.

*   *   *   *

Mitchell strolled to the store with his hands in his pockets. He despised shopping and only did it when he had to, but his supplies were getting dangerously low. That was one drawback of not being married; having to fend for himself.

He was an awful cook and had Widow Cooper from the house across the road from his workshop make him three loaves of bread per week. In return, he fixed things for her. She was in her sixties and all alone. Mitchell was more than happy to help her, and in all honesty, he enjoyed her company. It was nice to have a woman in his life with no strings attached, and she reminded him of his mother.

But Mrs. Cooper couldn't do all the cooking for him. He had to look after himself. He groaned as he climbed the stairs to the store.

"Morning, Mitch, what brings you here on a Saturday morning?" Brian Gibson greeted him.

He shrugged. "Run out of cheese and jam."

Archie chuckled. "You know you ought to add other things to your diet."

"I would, but I can't cook a lick, you know that. I eat at the café often enough, but if I do that all the time, I'll go broke."

"I understand. I guess that's the delight of having a wife, having someone to cook for you." Archie grimaced as soon as he finished that sentence.

Mitch sighed. "I was supposed to be married, remember? I wasn't counting on having to fend for myself for this long."

Archie touched his arm. "I'm sorry. I shouldn't rub it in. But you know, you don't have to be alone. There are plenty of lovely young women in this town?"

Mitchell sighed. "I'm not over Miranda yet. Besides, if she couldn't love me the way I am, who can?"

Brian frowned and gripped his shoulder. "I'm sorry she broke your heart, but not all women are like that. It saddens us, and we are disappointed with how it turned out; we want you to find happiness, Mitch. We feel like you're family, and we just want you to be happy."

Mitch sighed. "Thank you. But I'm better off alone. Can't get hurt again if I don't let anyone in."

Archie frowned. "What makes you think you'll get hurt if you let someone in?"

Mitch shrugged. "I'm not a whole man anymore. The best I can offer a woman is a broken-down old cripple, unsteady on my feet. I'll never be able to run properly, play ball with my children, or climb a tree to rescue a kite. I'll never be able to dance with my wife, at least not well. What kind of a man does that make me? What

139

kind of woman would want that? Not even Miranda wanted me once I was damaged goods."

"Mitch, that isn't true. Miranda was the one who lost out there; she chose the man with wealth and everything going for him, and look how that turned out. None of that stuff matters at the end of the day. I believe someone will love you for your heart." Archie squeezed his shoulder.

"Thank you, but I'm just better off alone." Mitchell shrugged. "I better get my jam and cheese." He wandered towards the shelves.

Archie looked up at his father. "Miranda really broke his heart."

"Yes, I'm so disappointed she did that, broke a good man in two. It was her leaving him that broke him, not losing a leg."

"I agree. We better step up the prayers."

"Yeah."

"Clara and I have been trying to share the gospel with him, hoping to get him to attend church. He needs the Lord more than ever."

"Yeah, let's continue praying for him." Brian nodded to Issy Fletcher, who hurried in the door. She never did anything slowly. She flew in like a whirlwind.

Archie raised his brows at his father. "A woman like that would do Mitch some good."

"She's awfully spunky."

"That's why she'd be perfect for him. Really wake him up."

"Well, pray; who knows what God might do."

"Clara has it covered." Archie raised his brows and chuckled.

"Watch out!" Mitch's words were too late. Issy hurried around the corner, focused on the shelves, and crashed right into him. He toppled on his feet and fell back on the ground. She fell, too, and both lost what was in their arms. Mitch sat up, horrified to see his trouser leg had ridden up and some of the wood was exposed. He quickly yanked his trousers back down and stood to his feet.

Issy sat up and put a hand to her head.

"Are you okay, Miss Fletcher?"

Issy gripped her head with her other hand. "I'm okay; my head is spinning."

"I'm not surprised. You hit me pretty hard."

She opened her eyes as her head began to clear. Her cheeks reddened, and she bit her lip. "I'm sorry, Mr. Sullivan, I didn't mean to; I wasn't thinking."

"Hey, no harm done." Mitchell put a hand out to her to help her up. She smiled, took his hand, and stood; he placed a hand on her back and ensured she was steady on her feet.

"That was most kind of you, and thank you for understanding."

He grinned and bent down to pick up their spilled items, placing hers in her basket. "You are most welcome. Would you allow me to carry this for you while you finish shopping?" Mitchell was amused at his own words.

Issy's cheeks reddened even more. "Thank you." She smiled, and there was that freckle. "It might be safer." She chuckled.

Mitchell gulped. "It would be my pleasure." He observed Issy, she was completely disheveled; her hair half-falling out of its pins, wisping around her face. Fighting the urge to tuck some of it behind her ear, he chuckled internally. It occurred to him that even her earlobe had freckles on it. His heart lurched; her freckles were so appealing—so much a part of her character.

She blushed. "What? Do I have something on my face?"

"There is a smudge on your cheek. Will you allow me?"

She nodded, so he pulled his handkerchief from his pocket and brushed gently at her cheek, then impulsively tucked a wayward tendril of auburn hair behind her ear. She gasped and closed her eyes.

He withdrew his hand abruptly. "I'm sorry; please forgive me."

She opened her eyes, and they shone. His touch had been so gentle, and it set her heart to racing, she could hear it pounding in her ears. Her feelings for him had been growing for a time. It wasn't like the other crushes she'd had. There was something about him that made her head spin and her heart flutter. She looked shyly at the ground and blushed. "That's okay, Mr. Sullivan; you just... caught me by surprise." She looked at him shyly.

"It was over the line, and I'm sorry, Miss Fletcher. if you wish me to leave you alone, I will." He held her basket out for her to take.

Instead, she smiled and slipped her hand under his outstretched arm. "No, I may need you to guide me in case I fall again." She looked at him shyly.

His heart flipped, and he inadvertently let out a gasp and smiled at her. "It'll be my pleasure, Miss Fletcher. I'll make sure you don't fall." *What is happening? Mitch, you cannot let yourself fall for a woman.*

"Please call me Issy; we're friends, aren't we?" She shrugged. "At least, I think we are."

He grinned at her and locked his eyes on hers. "We are friends, Issy, and please, I'm just Mitch, or some people even call me Sully."

"Mitch is just fine; I like that name. Well, Mitch, we both have shopping to do. Shall we get on with it?"

"Sure. You lead me." He gave her a sideways smile.

Issy chuckled. "Alright. Is that all you're getting?"

"Yeah, I pretty well live on cheese and jam." He shrugged one shoulder.

"That's not much of a meal."

Mitch grimaced. "I can't cook for peanuts."

Issy returned his grimace. "I'm not a whole lot better, but I'm improving. I'm hoping someone will want to buy my boxed lunch?"

"Boxed lunch?"

"Don't you know?" She added a box of cinnamon to the basket.

"No." Mitchell shook his head and creased his brows.

"I guess you'd have no reason to, not being at the church or having children at the school. Our town is really growing, and the school is getting overcrowded, the church too. They plan to add another classroom, and the church is helping since they meet in the schoolhouse. The extra space will benefit the school and the church."

Mitchell nodded, surprisingly her incessant chatter no longer bothered him. "What's the lunch got to do with it?"

Issy added a tin of peas and five potatoes to the basket. They turned up another aisle. "We're fundraising. The town coffers don't have nearly enough for the job. So, we're having a boxed lunch auction. All the women over sixteen who want to will make a lunch all wrapped up, and the men bid on them anonymously. If you win the lunch, you get to eat with the woman who made it."

"Sounds interesting."

"Course Ma told Pa what her basket looks like, so he knows which one to pick; she has to put in enough for all the children."

"I see. When is this happening?" Mitchell wasn't sure why he was asking these questions, except that she was so easy to talk to and he found her intriguing.

They strolled down another aisle, and Issy gathered five large apples and added them to her basket. "Tomorrow after the church service. Why don't you come? It would be fun, and it's for a good cause."

He screwed up his face. "I'm not sure. I don't usually go to church." *Seek Me, and you will find Me.* He gasped at the voice in his soul.

Issy didn't notice; she was busy inspecting the onions to choose the one she wanted. "It would be nice to see you there if you come. Of course, if you do, make sure

144

you bring plenty of money and get yourself a big lunch. It's for a good cause."

"I'll think about it."

"Well, I think this is all I need. You've been a real gentleman; you are now free of your obligation." Issy slipped her hand out from Mitchell's arm and grinned at him. That freckle appeared again.

Mitch felt his heart flip. "It's fine; I'll make sure you get to the counter safe and sound; I can't have you tripping over your feet." He found himself scrambling for a reason to spend more time with her. *Careful Mitchell, you cannot afford to get attached. It'll only lead to heartache again.*

"Thank you." She linked her hand under his arm again.

They continued to chat as they ambled to the counter. He was glad she was on the side that had his good leg. Maybe she wouldn't notice the limp so much or hear the occasional squeak from the metal hinges on his artificial leg.

As they turned towards the counter, Archie spotted them. He and his father shared a knowing glance. "Hello, you two?" Archie raised his brows at Mitchell.

Mitch blushed deeply. "I'm just escorting Miss Fletcher. I bumped into her and inadvertently knocked her down. It's the least I could do." He tried to keep his voice gruff and casual as though it was completely normal.

Issy smiled. It was nice of him to take the blame.

"I see." Archie grinned. "Now, what have you got there, Miss Fletcher?"

She removed her hand from Mitch's arm and took back her basket. She put it on the counter and made her purchases.

Mitch stood back, holding his two items, and waited. Issy paid her money and turned to smile at him. "Thank you, Mitch, and have a good day; I hope I see you tomorrow." She lifted her basket off the counter; and he noticed it had three yellow flowers stitched on the front of the white wicker.

He nodded to her, and Archie noticed a twinkle in his eye. He looked at Mitch and raised his brows. "That makes me happy."

"What?"

"You escorting Miss Fletcher."

"You're reading something that isn't there, Arch; I told you, I knocked her down, and I was just being neighborly."

Archie nodded and gave his father a knowing look. "Okay, whatever you say."

"Just these two things, and charge them, please," Mitchell mumbled. His old surliness returned.

Archie chuckled. *Whenever she is around, he lights up.* "Yes. Of course."

He made his purchases and hurried home as fast as his wooden leg would allow. It was in agony, his leg had twisted a little when he fell, and one of the metal braces was poking him. He couldn't wait to take it off, it would require some mending that evening.

Seventeen

Mitchell had no explanation for why he arose early, bathed, and dressed in his nice shirt and one pair of suit trousers. It only just hid the metal braces and leather straps of his prosthetic leg. He grimaced, hoping they wouldn't be noticeable, applied some cologne and left his cabin.

Almost automatically, he strode to the church and walked up the stairs. He was inside before he realized where he was. He gulped and looked around. He hadn't been there since Miranda left him. They'd attended together all the time. Michell had never taken it seriously; he'd just gone because she asked him to.

He trembled slightly and slipped into a chair at the back of the room in the far corner, hoping no one would notice him. Most people were already there, chatting amongst themselves while they waited for Reverend Cross to start the service.

It was all a blur until the Reverend's words pierced his mind. The pastor lifted the Bible and read. "Come unto Me, all ye that labor and are heavy laden, and I will give ye rest. Take My yoke upon you and learn of Me; for I am meek and lowly in heart: and ye shall find rest unto your souls."

Mitchell gasped without meaning to and closed his eyes. *I want to find that rest, God. Will You show me?* He thought about the words for a time, his mind drifting back to his friends' comments about finding peace in his soul. He would find a way to seek it.

Mitchell drew his mind back to focus on the Reverend's words, he was praying a benediction over them all. Then he lowered his hands and smiled. "I hope you will all join us for the box lunch auction." At his signal two men walked out to the office space at the back of the church and carried in a large table with a variety of different sized boxes and baskets on it.

Mitchell grinned as he noticed a white wicker basket with three yellow flowers stitched on the front.

Sheriff Connor stood. "I'm your auctioneer for the event." He moved through each basket; most were purchased by husbands, and families walked away together to share their lunches.

Then came the baskets of the single ladies, and the young men bartered back and forth. Mitch sat in silence in the back row, and no one paid him any mind. At last, the sheriff came to the white wicker basket with three yellow flowers on the front. He smiled and reached his hand in his pocket and pulled out a handful of coins.

"Who'll give me ten cents for this lovely basket?" the sheriff called.

A person near the front offered ten, another fifteen, still another twenty. The bidding was furious as it had been for all the boxes, and it reached one dollar and ten cents. Young men turned out their pockets and shook their heads in defeat. Just as the auctioneer was about to present it to Timothy Armstrong, the highest bidder, Mitch called out, "Two dollars."

All faces spun around to see where the voice had come from, but he was behind the crowd, and no one noticed him. Issy blushed. Most had gone for less than a dollar.

She hoped whoever it was, wouldn't be disappointed that the food wasn't very good, and the company was her.

"Any advances on two dollars?"

The other young men shrugged and shook their heads in defeat. The sheriff lifted the basket. "Come out, whoever you are; the basket is yours for two dollars." Issy bit her lip and raised her brow, hoping it wasn't some old man.

Mitch stood slowly and walked to the front. There was a collective gasp. No one had seen Mitchell Sullivan in church for a very long time, and certainly not as tidy as he looked that day.

Issy's cheeks colored, and she looked at the floor. Sheriff Connor raised his brows. "Well, Mr. Sullivan, come and take your prize. Would the woman whose basket this is stand up."

Issy stood out of her seat and wandered over to Mitchell. He winked at her, offered her his arm, and led her to the seats to wait. He was baffled at his own actions. His mind knew it was foolhardy to get close to a woman, it would only set himself up for heartache. But it seemed his heart overruled every time and he found himself drawn to Issy whether he liked it or not.

Neither looked at each other or said a word until the auction was finished. The chairs were pushed back, and people spread around the room to eat. Mitch led Issy over to a table in the corner. He struggled to get up and down off the floor without drawing attention to his leg, so he gestured to the table, seated her and took the seat at the end of the table adjacent to her.

He placed the basket on the table and smiled. "So, what tasty treats do you have for me today?" His heart raced, and he was quite unable to believe the pounding in his ears and swirling of his thoughts. *Come on Sullivan, get yourself under control. Issy is a friend and that's all she can ever be.* He tried to draw his feelings back into line, let his mind take over again rather than his heart.

She looked shyly up at him. The softness in his copper eyes made her blush. "Did you know it was my basket?"

"Mmmhmm." He winked at her.

"Why did you bid on it?" She lowered her eyes. "Why did you come today?"

He reached over and lifted her chin. "I just thought I'd like to have lunch with a pretty girl today."

Issy gulped and blushed even deeper. He was starting to sound like a suitor.

"Why?"

"What do you mean?" He frowned.

"Why me?"

Mitchell shrugged. "Don't know anyone else, 'sides, we're friends, aren't we?"

"Yes." She smiled, nodded, and turned to open the basket. "I'm sorry, my cooking isn't any good." She screwed up her nose.

"Hey, Issy, it'll be a lot better than mine." They sat together and ate the somewhat overcooked biscuits, chewy potatoes, and lumpy gravy. The beans were unevenly cooked, and they finished with an apple pie with a burnt bottom.

"I'm sorry, I burnt the bottom of it." She grimaced.

He winked at her. "Ma always said charcoal is good for your teeth."

"You're very kind."

"So are you." He fixed his eyes on her blue ones and gave her just the hint of a smile.

"Why did you come today?"

"I told you, for lunch?"

"But you were here for the service too. I saw you come in."

He shrugged. "Thought I'd check out what it was all about."

She grinned. "And?"

"And, I think I have some thinking to do. I'm a wretched and broken man, and I'm not sure God would be interested in me." He sighed.

Issy put a hand on his arm. "Oh, Mitchell, we are all wretched; none of us deserves God's love; that's the beauty of it. He offers His grace and mercy to even the most wretched sinners."

He nodded. "So, I'm beginning to learn."

"Won't you give your heart to Him?" Her eyes flooded with tears.

Mitchell squinted at her. "Why does it matter so much to you?"

"I don't want to see anyone suffer; all souls are precious to God."

He grimaced. "I'm just not sure I can believe like you do."

"I've been praying for you."

"Thank you."

"You're welcome."

"And thank you for the lunch; I enjoyed it."

"You flatter me; it wasn't much good. I'm sorry." Issy screwed up her nose.

"Hey, don't run yourself down; it was great. I enjoyed the food and the company." He smiled and squeezed her arm.

"Thank you." She blushed and busied herself with cleaning up.

He helped her and stood to leave. "Do you need a ride home?"

"No, I can go with my parents, thank you though. I hope to see you in town sometime."

He nodded, and she turned to follow her family out the door.

* * * *

Mitchell paced back and forth in his living room, wrestling with what he'd learned that day. He could no longer deny that it was more than attraction with Issy. "But I can't let myself love her; love only ends in hurt. I tried that once, and look where it left me." He sighed and hung his head.

He thought about Issy and then about Miranda. "I simply can't let myself be hurt again. I can't do it." He shuddered. "I'd rather be alone all my days than be hurt like that again."

Mitchell strolled out of the house. He needed to think; he needed to work out what was going on with God, with Miranda and the grip she still had on his heart, and with Issy, who was growing on him whether he liked it or not.

* * * *

"So, what do you make of that?" Wallace squinted at his daughter.

Issy lifted her head and frowned at her father across the table. "What do you mean?"

"Sullivan purchased your lunch. I assume he knew it was yours?" Wallace raised his brows.

She blushed. "Yes, he knew it was mine."

"So, what do you make of that?"

"Please don't be so cryptic; say what you mean." She put down her coffee cup. Her mother was resting off another headache, and all her siblings were reading in their rooms; they usually rested on a Sunday afternoon.

Wallace smiled. She always did prefer the forthright approach. He raised his brows. "You love him, don't you?"

Issy sucked in a deep breath, and her cheeks glowed red hot. She looked down at her cup and bit her lips together.

Wallace reached across and lifted her chin. "Daughter, you love him, don't you?" He smiled and his kind eyes held no judgement.

She nodded, and tears flooded her eyes.

"I thought so; I've never seen you so bashful; this isn't like the other crushes you've had." Both drank their coffee in silence for a time. Wallace put down his cup. "Does he love you?"

"Oh, Pa, I don't know. How do you know? It's not something you ask a man. Sometimes I feel like he does, and lately, he's warmed up to me, but he's got such a tortured soul... and oh, I don't know."

"I suspect if he paid two dollars for your basket lunch, he might." Wallace squeezed her hand.

"Or he just likes food."

Wallace's brows shot up and he gave her a sideways grin. "Your food? He knew it was yours, he knows you don't cook very well, yet he paid two dollars for your box."

Issy gave him a wry smile. "Thanks, Pa, for your vote of confidence in me."

"You have so many talents, Darling. So, cooking doesn't come naturally to you, but you'll learn, and it's obvious he doesn't care. He ate every bite." Her father gestured to the empty basket on the counter.

She shrugged. "I don't know what to think; I know he's not a believer, Pa; he wants to be. I can see how he's agonizing over it. He was crushed by his fiancée leaving I'm not sure he knows how he feels."

"Then you can only pray."

"I have been. Extensively!"

Silence fell over them again and Issy focused on her cup. "How do you feel about him, Pa?"

"Look at me, Issy."

She looked up at him shyly and bit her lip. Wallace gripped both of her hands and smiled kindly. "I like him very much, and I would give you my blessing wholeheartedly. I just have one concern."

"Oh?"

"Well, two, actually. He's not a believer, and he's not over his fiancée, is he?"

"I don't know."

"I think you need to talk to him, be upfront. Men appreciate that. You know men are often afraid to tell women how we feel. Maybe if you're honest with him, he'll be honest with you."

She nodded. "I think it's going to need a lot of prayer."

"I agree. Your ma and I are praying for you. We just want you to be happy. If he makes you happy and can work through his brokenness, you'll have our blessing."

"Thank you. Could we pray now? I value your wisdom."

"Absolutely, Darling."

Wallace squeezed her hand, and they bowed their heads.

Eighteen

For a reason he couldn't place, Mitchell made his way to the house he'd built across town. He paused, sighed, opened the door, and walked inside. Brian Gibson had organized for it to be completed while he was still in recovery, but he'd never been to see it. There were too many painful memories.

He looked around. His mind spun as a hundred memories of Miranda flooded his brain all at once. Falling back onto the couch, he put his hands over his face, and let the memories overwhelm him. His mind swirled as he relived their courtship and engagement. The little flirtations that had started as innocent conversations at the store or in town; the first dance he'd taken her to and the way her golden hair had shone in the lamplight. The way she'd smiled at him and refused to dance with anyone else; the picnic they'd had by the lake when he proposed to her.

The look on her face when he'd brought her to the house he was building; her delight as he took her by the hand and showed her every room—her squeals of joy at the stone fireplaces and handmade furniture.

Mitchell lifted his head and wiped his eyes. Looking around, he sucked in painful breaths, letting his heart feel every moment of the pain. He stood and walked to the fireplace, reached up to the mantle, and picked up the photograph she'd placed there. It was the two of them on the day they'd got engaged.

He closed his eyes and let the moment come drifting back to his mind.

"What have you got behind your back?" he asked.

"A photograph." Miranda grinned at him.

"A photograph of what?"

"Here, open it and look." She passed it to him.

He grinned, stroked her cheek, opened the envelope, and slipped out the photograph. "Oh, it's our engagement photo."

"Yes."

He furrowed his brows. "I love it, of course, but why have you brought it here today?"

"Because the house is almost finished, and we get married in a little over a month. I wanted this to be our first piece of us in this house, christen it, so to speak." She flashed him that wide smile that caused the dimples to show on her cheeks.

He brushed back a tendril of blonde hair from her face and kissed her. "It's a thoughtful gift; where shall we put it?"

Miranda looked around. "Eventually, on the wall, but since there is still work to do, why not put it up on the mantel? It'll be the first thing people see when they walk into the house."

He smiled, put it on the mantel, took her in his arms, and kissed her. "I love you so much; I can't wait to be married to you."

"Me either. You know I love you, right? There is nothing you could ever do to stop me from loving you."

He grinned and cupped her cheek. "Me either; you're so beautiful and sweet."

"And you're so handsome and strong, everything I want in a man...."

Mitchell snapped out of the memory, and anger filled his heart. Less than a month later, she'd left him. He lifted the matchbox off the mantle, struck one, lit the photo's corner, threw it in the fireplace, and watched it curl up and burn. He added some kindling and started a small fire, then hung his head and let out a single sob. He squared his shoulders and took a deep breath. "Be done with you. I can't live with your memory anymore. I need to be free of you."

He looked around. The entire house was full of memories of her. "I could never live here, not alone or with another person, while her ghost haunts the place. I have to be free of her." He sniffed back another sob. "I have to find a way to get you out of my head. You're gone; you betrayed me, so why do I still love you?" He shouted. He punched out at the wall. "God, if You're there, I need to get Miranda out of my heart and head. If I'm to have any chance of finding happiness again, as Clara suggested."

He wasn't quite ready to admit he loved Issy, at least not out loud. He certainly felt something for her, but he wasn't free to do so even if he could admit it. Not while Miranda still held so tight a grip on his heart.

"How do I free myself of you?" Mitchell shouted again. "How do I get you out of my heart?" Burning the photo had been cathartic, but he couldn't burn the house down. He had two choices, sell the house, or find a way to get her memory out of it.

He looked around; she had chosen the curtains and the couches; she'd made the rugs and chosen the wallpaper he'd forked out a fortune for. He grimaced. She'd insisted they go to Ravensfield and explore the shops till she found the suitable wallpaper—a pale blue with white flowers.

He walked up to the wall; in one place, the paper was coming loose where the glue hadn't stuck properly. He slipped his hand under it, tore a massive chunk of the wallpaper away, screwed it up and threw it into the fireplace.

"That's what I'll do. I'll change the house; I'll get every inch of Miranda out of it. Maybe then I'll be free to move on from her." Mitchell began to frantically pull at strips of wallpaper; it came off in large chunks and all went straight into the fire.

He looked around, picked up one of the rugs that Miranda had made, and thrust it into the flames.

Why did I come here? Why is it now that I'm so determined to get rid of her?

He stared into the flames while they consumed the rug. Clara had dared to suggest it was Issy that he had feelings for. "Do I? Is that why I'm here? Do I want to get Miranda out so I can let Issy in?" he asked the fire. But then he thought about Issy finding out about his leg and running out of the room in horror, when she realized he was not a whole man.

He punched out at the wall. "Why God?" If not for his accident, he and Miranda would have been married and living happily together.

But what had she said? "*You know I love you, right? There is nothing you could do to stop me from loving you.*"

"But it was a lie. Something did stop you. I don't understand; I would have loved you with no legs, or if you got burned by fire because it wasn't your body that I loved you for, it was your heart...."

He bit his lips together. "I thought that's why you loved me too. But obviously, me being physically whole mattered to you a great deal."

Mitchell allowed his thoughts to turn to Issy. He'd never been so intrigued by freckles before. Part of him wished to know if the freckles on her hands and wrists went all the way up her arms. He blushed and thought of the freckle on her lip. Was it her looks that he was attracted to? He could admit that much; he was undoubtedly attracted to her. Was it just intrigue because she was so unique, or was there more to it than that?

But how could he be attracted to two women who were so different? Miranda was always so carefully groomed. She seldom had a hair out of place and didn't like to get dirty. She was sweet and delicate. "What did she ever see in a dirty blacksmith anyway?" He frowned. He was always filthy at the end of the day, with char from his forge or iron shavings, any number of things all over him. But then Miranda had never come to his work or spent time with him until he had cleaned himself up.

Mitchell squinted. Was she really that interested in physical appearance? Was that why she went for Jones? He was a good-looking man, tall, broad, and wealthy. Perhaps she was shallower than he thought. He sighed and shrugged as the last of the rug burned up. "Did her leaving me actually do me a favor? I hate to think that of her, but Clara said all things work out for good. Was I not meant to be with her? Am I meant to be with Issy instead? Oh, but I can't; I can't let her know about my leg." He groaned loudly and punched out at the mantle.

He couldn't help but smile as his mind turned to Issy again. She couldn't be more different than Miranda. She had flyaway hair, and tresses of auburn always hung around her face, the pins always working loose. She hadn't been worried to see him working, with dirt and grime all over him. He remembered her sitting on the upturned pail in his workshop and talking his ear off while he worked, not caring that he was sweaty and filthy.

A wide smile crossed Mitchell's face. She loved to climb trees, often donned rubber boots, and helped her father and brothers on the farm. He'd been around to their estate several times to fix things, and when Issy wasn't working, she'd be there pulling flowers or even wrangling calves. He chuckled as he remembered seeing her galloping Pixie headlong past the town and toward her home with her bonnet pushed back from her head, and her auburn hair working its way loose.

Now that he thought about it, Issy seemed to appear in his life a lot. His mind swirled and he fell back into the chair, and turned his mind to the sermon that morning. "Come unto Me all ye who are heavy laden, and I will give ye rest," he spoke the words aloud.

"God, I want that rest! How do I seek it?" He stood abruptly, left the house, and walked straight to Clara and Archie's home.

Clara answered his knock at the door. "Mitchell? Whatever is the matter?"

Mitchell gasped and struggled to hold back his emotions. "I need to find that rest, Clara; I need God's peace in my life."

"Oh, Mitch." Clara embraced him. "Please come in."

He nodded and walked inside. He paced back and forth as Clara put the coffeepot on. Archie entered the room and looked quizzically at Clara and then at Mitch.

He walked towards his friend. "Mitch?"

Mitchell could no longer keep back the tears. He fell against Archie and sobbed. Archie put an arm around him and let the man cry. This was anguish from his soul; it took a lot to make a tough man like Mitch cry.

When he finally stood back, Mitch swiped at his eyes with his handkerchief.

"Do you want me to pray with you, Mitch?"

"Would you? I want to find that peace you spoke of. I'm tired of living in my wretchedness. The pastor spoke of finding rest. Can you help me?"

Archie sniffed away his own tears. "Absolutely, my friend."

He gestured to the table, and Clara joined them with full coffee cups. Archie pulled his Bible from the shelf and took Mitch into the Scriptures. They spent more than an hour going through the gospel and God's plan to send Christ for the redemption of sinners. Clara prayed without ceasing, for Mitch to find the peace his soul craved.

With the help of his friends, he sobbed out his repentance and pain before the Lord. He prayed for forgiveness and turned his life over to the Living God.

At last, Mitch lifted his head, and his eyes flooded with tears. He smiled and closed his eyes. Taking a deep breath, he opened his eyes and grinned.

"That's the peace of the Lord, my friend. He doesn't fix your problems, but He bears them with you." Archie gripped his shoulder.

"I've never felt so light. I still have no idea what my future holds, but I no longer feel filled with torment. What do I do now?"

Archie passed him the Bible. "I want you to have this; read it each day and fill your heart and mind with it. If you want me to, I'll read it with you, and we can help each other understand it."

"How could I help you? I don't know the first thing about the Bible."

"Yes, but you have the Holy Spirit with you. His job is to help you grow and to sanctify you. He'll guide you, and I'll walk alongside you too. We're really brothers now, Mitch. In the family of God."

Mitch raised his brows and nodded. He left their home and walked outside, stopping abruptly in his tracks. "She's gone." He smiled. "I'm free of her." He nearly collapsed as a wave of overwhelming love for Issy washed over him. He closed his eyes and sighed loudly. "But I can never act on that love, the minute she sees my leg she'll run. All I can ask for is to love her from afar." He shook his head and sighed loudly. Thrusting his hands in his pockets he headed for his cabin.

Nineteen

Issy looked at her father. "Thanks, Pa; I feel better knowing it's in the Lord's hands. I'm afraid to speak to Mitch. What if I'm wrong and he's just a friend?"

"Then you're no worse off by being honest."

"And if he rejects me."

"Darling, the Lord is with you, no matter what happens."

"You're right, of course. If he rejects me, then the Lord doesn't want us together. I just hope if that happens we can remain friends." She sighed. "I think I'll go find him and speak to him now."

"I'll be here praying for you, Darling."

"Thank you. I'm gonna need it. This is 'bout the scariest thing I've ever done, in all my life."

He stood and embraced her. "Just remember loving someone makes you vulnerable and leaves you open to the potential of being hurt. But if he loves you, it'll be worth it in the end."

"Thanks, Pa."

Issy saddled Pixie and galloped to town, praying all the way. Her heart pounded and she took deep breaths. For all her confidence, she'd never been good with matters of the heart. She felt incredibly vulnerable, but honesty was always the best way, she expected it from others, and she tried to live it herself.

Pausing at Mitchell's cabin door she took a deep breath. *Give me the words and the boldness to say them, Lord.* No one was home. She frowned and sighed.

"Perhaps it's not meant to be." She turned to walk away and spotted Mitch walking toward her with his hands in his pockets and a book under his arm. She patted her tethered horse and ran to him. "Mitch."

He turned to look at her, swiped at his eyes and smiled. "Issy, what are you doing here?"

"Looking for you?"

"Why?" He frowned.

"I don't know what I'm doing, but I know I'd like to talk. Is there a place we could go?"

"It's not too cold; we could go out to the chair at The Glade; it's in the open but away from others."

She smiled. "That's good." She was glad he respected her reputation. It wouldn't do for them to have this conversation behind closed doors. He moved the Bible to his left arm and offered her his right. She smiled and took it. His heart lurched with the joy of having her on his arm, but he swallowed back those feelings. *It's not worth it, Mitch, she's just a friend. It's better that way for both of us.*

They walked in silence until they came to the wooden chair. Both took a seat and Mitchell turned to look at her. "What do you want to talk about?"

Issy blushed and then noticed the Bible. "Why do you have a Bible with you?"

He grinned. "Issy, you were right. I found peace in the Lord today. Just now, Clara and Archie led me through the Gospel."

"Ohhhh!" Without thinking, she threw her arms around his neck. "That is wonderful news. Oh, Mitchell, I'm so glad." She pulled back from him; a deep blush grew on her cheeks. "I'm sorry. I just get carried away with my emotions sometimes."

"Don't be. I love that you wear your heart on your sleeve like that." He couldn't keep the grin off his face, his practical mind failing to keep his heart from overruling.

"I've never seen your eyes so bright. It looks like you've found peace for your soul."

He grinned, and his face shone with joy. "Yes." He paused and looked her in the eye. "And I've finally been able to put Miranda behind me, once and for all. She no longer has a grip on my heart. The Lord has helped me to release her."

Issy gripped his arm with both her hands and gasped. "Oh, that's wonderful." Her eyes filled with tears. "I'm so happy for you."

"What's with the tears?" He gently brushed an escapee from her cheek.

Her lips trembled. "Will you allow me to be honest and share my heart with you? I'm terrified to do so, but the Lord is with me, and He gives me courage."

"Absolutely." Mitchell gulped. "You can tell me anything. We're friends, remember." He raised his brows at her.

"That's the thing...." She paused and bit her lips together. Hanging her head, she toyed with her hands in her lap. "I like you a lot."

"I like you a lot, too." He smiled.

"No, I mean a lot, as in, I think I love you." Her voice quivered.

Mitchell gasped. "You think you love me?" His heart began to race. *No, Mitchell, you absolutely cannot allow yourself to love her.* He squashed those feelings deep down inside. It was merely a pipe dream.

She raised terrified eyes to meet his, desperate to read in them that he reciprocated her feelings. "I know women aren't supposed to be so forward, but Pa told me to be honest so, yes. I love you." Her lips trembled, and her breathing sped up.

Mitchell closed his eyes. *She can't know about my leg.* He stood up and walked two steps away. "I want to let myself love you, Issy."

"You want to? Why can't you?"

"I'm afraid you'll reject me. I can't go through that again." He sucked in a loud breath, forcing his feelings into line.

"What are you talking about?"

He turned. "There is something you don't know about me, and when you find out, you'll want nothing to do with me." His face curled up in agony. "You'll run for the hills."

"What do you mean?" She tipped her head to the side and frowned.

He thrust his hands in his pockets and looked at his feet. "I'm not a complete man; I'm broken."

"We're all broken, Mitch."

"No." He sighed and whispered a prayer for strength. "You were honest with me; you deserve me to be honest with you." He lifted his head. She remained seated but looked at him in anticipation. He closed his eyes. "When I say I'm broken, I mean physically. I'll understand if you want to walk away. I'll never be a complete man; I'll never be totally whole and able to be what you need." He trembled and turned his back. He walked two steps away. "That's why I can't let myself love you. You don't deserve to end up with half a man."

Issy closed her eyes and took a deep breath. "Are you saying that because of your wooden leg?"

He gasped and turned to face her. "You know? How do you know?"

"Yes, I know. The man in the store told Pa, and he told me."

Mitch's face fell. "How long have you known?"

"Since the day you removed the gates, and you slipped over."

Tears flooded his eyes. "You've never mentioned it."

She stood up and walked to him, stopping a few feet before him. "Of course not."

"Why not? Doesn't it repulse you? Don't you feel like I'm half a man? Like I'm broken, nothing more than a cripple? How could you love me if you know that?" A tear streaked down his cheek.

Issy dropped her head for a moment, then lifted it and closed the gap between them. She took a deep breath and put a hand on his cheek, brushing off the tear with her thumb. "Mitchell Sullivan. I've never mentioned your leg because I don't care a fig about how many legs you have. That's not why I love you." She looked him in the eye and flashed him a wide smile. There was the freckle on her lip.

Mitchell's heart was doing somersaults. "Really? You could love me with one leg?" He let out a single sob and sucked in another loud breath. His mind swirled and overwhelming hope grew in his heart.

She chuckled and dropped her hand from his face. "I'd love you with no legs; it's your heart, your character that impresses me. You're the kindest man I know. You pretend to be all gruff and surly, but I know you're gentle and tender-hearted. I've seen how you are with Tillie, and I know it was you that gave me the sewing machine." She raised her brows and tipped her head to the side, smiling wryly.

He blushed deeply and raised his brows. "How do you know?"

"It has your mark on it, the hanging S. I dropped something down the back, pushed the machine out to get it, and saw the S. It's the same as on the gates and the things in your workshop, so I knew it was you."

"For how long?" Mitchell furrowed his brow. It was becoming increasingly difficult to rein in the hope and joy that bubbled up in his heart.

"It was when I was making you the coat."

He dropped his mouth open. "You knew when you gave me the coat that I had given you the sewing machine?"

She smiled. "Yes, you aren't nearly as mysterious as you think. Why did you give it to me?"

He shrugged and scratched his chin. "I'm not sure; I think in some way I was drawn to you; I hadn't allowed myself to love you, partly because I wasn't free of Miranda and partly because I was certain you couldn't love a cripple." He scowled and hung his head.

Issy gripped his arm. Her eyes became intense, and she fixed him with a stare that nearly made his knees buckle. "Mitchell, the only part of you that was crippled was your heart." She grinned and put her hand on his chest; her heart pounded in her ears, and she prayed for courage. "But I can see that's healed now. I don't need you to have both legs. I just need your heart. You're not crippled, you're a strong and incredible man, and I'm afraid I've fallen in love with you. I'm sorry if my forthrightness frightens you. I just prefer honesty." Issy gave him a shy smile and lowered her head.

Mitch grinned his slow toothy grin and reached his large hand out to lift her chin. She looked up and smiled at him.

He touched a spot on her lip with his thumb. "Did you know you have a freckle on your lip, right here?"

She furrowed her brow. "Do I?"

"Yes, but I can only see it when you smile, and every time I've seen it, all I've wanted to do is kiss your soft lips."

She blushed and tucked her lips under. He cupped her cheek. "Issy, I've never met anyone who looks like you. Wild red hair, all these freckles." He examined her face with his eyes.

"I know. I'm so ugly." Issy hung her head.

He gasped and lifted her chin again. "Oh no, you couldn't be more wrong. You're striking. I love your freckles. Whenever you smile and lift your cheeks, the freckles dance, and it's so endearing. I keep hoping to get a glimpse of the freckle on your lip, and you have them on your earlobe, too." He gently touched her lobe.

"It's the most beautiful feature I've seen in a woman." He reached for her hands and rubbed his thumbs over them. "I love that these hands have freckles. I kinda wanna know if they go all the way up your arms and over the rest of your body." He blushed and chuckled. "It's like God has decorated you, like a beautiful, speckled egg."

Tears streamed from her eyes. "Oh, Mitchell. No one has ever liked my freckles before; the boys at school teased me. They called me freckle face and told me I was ugly."

He smiled and brushed her cheek with the back of his fingers and fixed his eyes on her. She smiled slowly, and he ran his finger across her lip and stopped at the freckle. "I'm in love with you, Freckle Face." He grinned.

"I'm in love with you, too." She smiled back at him; her eyes sparkled.

"Issy."

"Yes." Her cheeks were an endearing red.

He tucked some hair behind her ear. "You've redeemed me; you've awakened my soul. Well, you and God."

"I'm so glad." She put both hands on his chest.

He wrapped his arms around her and held her close, laying his head against hers. "I am finally free."

"Free?" she murmured, relishing being in his arms.

"Free from the darkness in my soul, free from my lost love and broken heart. And best of all, free to love you, and I plan to do so for the rest of my days." He pulled back and lifted her chin. "If you'll let me?"

She lifted her shining eyes to him. "Of course, I will."

"Thank the Lord for His abundant blessings," Mitchell observed her with his eyes for a time, a broad smile crossed his face. Issy smiled back at him, her eyes glistened, and that freckle tantalized him. She slipped her arms around his neck, and he lowered his head till their lips met in a tender kiss.

THE END

About the Author

Jo Dawson grew up on a dairy farm in Wellsford, a small town in the North Island of New Zealand. She spent fifteen years as a teacher in New Zealand and abroad before becoming a stay-at-home mum and completing her graduate degree in Theology.

She has lived in Australia and the USA for a time, and these experiences have added to her love of people and history. Blessed with a vivid imagination and a love of classical literature and historical fiction, Jo virtually grew up best friends with Anne Shirley, romping with Jo March and her sisters, sailing a raft down the Mississippi with Huckleberry Finn or living in the 'little house' with Laura Ingalls.

Born and raised in a strong Christian family, Jo's faith is at the centre of who she is, with a lifetime of being involved in churches and Christian camps. These two loves; literature and the Lord, have inevitably converged into writing compelling stories of strong Christian women courageously facing the hardships of life on the frontier. It is her hope that women of all ages would find encouragement from her heroines' experiences that, while fiction, so often mirror even our modern lives.

Jo currently resides in the small North Island town of Waipu in New Zealand, where she lives with her husband, son, father-in-law and a very lazy cat.

Other books by J. L. Dawson

Journeys of the Heart Series
Awakening of the Heart
Shepherd of the Heart
Decisions of the Heart
A Home for the Heart
Blessings of the Heart
Legacies of the Heart

Douglas Falls Series
Prequel: The Cost of Duty
A Duty to Love
Twixt Duty and Love
A Duty to Family (coming soon)

Multiple Author Series (Standalone books).

Hers to Redeem Book 14: Aaron's Anguish
Hers to Redeem Book 18: Mitchell's Misfortune
Hers to Redeem Book 21: Robbie's Roaming

Standalone Books

To Love Nate – A Companion to Aaron's Anguish.

Where to find these books:
https://www.amazon.com/stores/J-L-Dawson/author
www.jodawsonauthor.com to sign up for my newsletter
jldawsonauthor@yahoo.com to write to the author
Jo Dawson and **J. L. Dawson Author**
-on Instagram and Facebook